TESS & THE ASHES CATASTROPHE

JENNI DOUGLASS

Thank you!
Jenni Douglass)

www.jennidouglasswrites.com

For my girls

1

PLAY

The umpire calls 'Play' to begin a match

It was the last ball and I needed two runs to win. I risked a glance at Eddie, who was ready to bowl. His team had won our last few matches and I knew he would do everything he could to win this one as well. He smirked, which did nothing to ease my nerves. Staring straight ahead, my hands gripped tight, waiting. It was now or never.

I've got this, I thought as I took a deep breath and squeezed even tighter.

The train lurched to a halt and my phone slipped from my grip. Watching my screen in disbelief, the ball crashed into my middle stump, sending the bails flying. *Noooo!*

On the Tube seat next to me, Eddie gave a victory cry. I glared at him, but he just shrugged before we both burst out laughing.

'Sorry, sweetheart, it's time to get off. Maybe you'll get him next time,' Dad said, giving Eddie a wink over my head.

Jumping off the train, I raced to the escalator so I could stand two steps above Eddie and, for once, look him in the eye. We chatted about the tactics for our rematch until we reached the top and exited St John's Wood station. As we walked to Lord's Cricket Ground, I looked up at the blue sky and couldn't see one single cloud. The weather people had said it would rain all day today and tomorrow for the start of the Test Match. Thank goodness they were wrong: cricketers hated rain, and I didn't want anything to spoil today.

As soon as Lord's came into view, Dad whipped out his phone and started taking a million photos. He totally looked like a tourist, so Eddie and I tried to stay a few steps behind him.

'Stop here,' Dad said, pointing to a stone frieze at the corner of the ground. 'I want to take a photo of you two.' Eddie and I groaned but Dad was having none of it. 'C'mon, Tess, this is your special day.'

'Fine!' I groaned again as I led Eddie to the frieze. Men and women holding lots of different sporting equipment were carved into the stone, and at the top it read 'Lord's Cricket Ground'. I was a bit confused by it, as I thought that only cricket was played at Lord's. Eddie gave me a sideways look and I knew he was thinking what I was thinking. Why were all these other sports there?

'Okay, smile and say "Ashes",' Dad said.

'Ashes,' Eddie and I mumbled as Dad clicked away.

Once Dad was satisfied that he'd taken enough photos, we continued down St John's Wood Road. When we finally reached the entrance gates, I was more nervous than I would have been going out to open the batting.

'These are called the "Grace Gates",' Dad said, surprising me with his knowledge. I thought he only knew about Australian cricket. 'They are named after W.G. Grace, one of England's greatest players.'

I strained my neck as he pointed to the massive stone pillar in between the two fancy black gates, and saw a dedication to William Gilbert Grace carved into the stone. Above that, his initials were also cut inside a stone wreath.

'What else can you see?' Dad asked.

'Ooh! There's a set of stumps!' Eddie cried out.

'Good spot!' Dad said, and Eddie beamed.

I turned my attention to the black iron gates either side of the pillars. They were so fancy, with the iron bent into curls and whorls. Underneath a yellow sun and red cricket ball, some of the metal was painted gold. Twisting my head left and right, I tried to work out why they were different.

'Are they letters?' I asked, turning to Dad.

'Yes, can you see what they say?'

Crinkling up my eyes, the letters finally came into focus. 'MCC?'

'That's right; they stand for Marylebone Cricket Club, which is the club the ground officially belongs to, although Middlesex County Cricket Club also play cricket here.'

Dad snapped a few more photos before we strolled through the gates. A huge stand rose high above, and Eddie and I gawped at the banners displaying some of cricket's legends. People were running everywhere carrying boxes of food and drink, setting up television cameras and shouting instructions into walkie-talkies, trying to get the ground ready for tomorrow's Test Match.

Up higher still, on top of a thin building, I could see a weathervane of an old man bent over a set of stumps. I turned to Dad to ask him if he knew what it was but stopped mid-sentence when I saw a silver bus pull up outside the Grace Gates. The sun reflected from the windows, stabbing my eyes, but as I squinted through the light, the bus door slid open and, like a god, my favourite player, dressed in Australian green and gold, emerged through a halo of sunrays. As I grabbed Eddie's arm in disbelief, he nodded next to me, perhaps wishing it was the England team bus instead, but still lost for words. Collecting their backpacks from the bus's luggage hold, the players turned and walked through the Grace Gates towards us.

I looked up at Dad, who grinned. 'Pretty cool, hey?' he said.

Cool? This was unbelievable.

'G'day,' Dad kept saying over and over as the players filed past us one by one, and most of the players nodded or said, 'G'day,' in reply. I couldn't speak. I only had eyes for one player. I couldn't believe that he was here. I mean, I knew I was going to meet the two captains today and that made me nervous enough. And Eddie and I had talked about the possibility that the other players might be at Lord's at the same time, but I never, ever dreamed I would see him. He walked closer and closer to me, and I felt my legs turn to jelly. And then he was only a few feet away from me. I almost melted on the spot when he looked directly at me, smiled, and said hello. I tried to smile back, I tried to speak, but I was so star-struck that my gaping mouth made me look like a total idiot. My mouth didn't close until the last Australian player had walked past. Inside I was screaming. This was the best day ever!

Eddie nudged me and whispered in my ear. 'Did you see what they were wearing?'

I nodded with a grin.

Last week, Mum had announced that if I was going to Lord's then I absolutely had to wear a dress. 'I will not have you looking like you've just stepped off a cricket ground,' Mum had insisted.

'But Mum, that's the point,' I'd replied, trying my best to keep my cool. 'Lord's *is* a cricket ground, so I should be wearing my cricket kit.'

'But Tess,' Mum had countered, 'as you keep reminding me, Lord's *is* the home of cricket, so you should want to look your *best*.'

'Mum! *All* the players will be in their *kit*.'

'That's because they are there to play cricket. You're there because you won a competition.'

'Urgh! It's so unfair! I hate wearing dresses,' I'd shouted at her before storming to my bedroom, slamming the door in protest. There had been absolutely no way I was going to wear a dress. I was a proper cricketer and proper cricketers always wore their kit, no matter what. Eddie and I had already discussed the matter and had agreed cricket kit was the only thing that could even be considered. The most difficult decision as far as we were concerned was which kit to wear. I'd really wanted to wear my Australian shirt and Eddie had wanted to wear his England one. In the end, we'd decided to wear our navy-blue club shirt and shorts so we'd look the same. Mum simply didn't get it. Luckily, Dad came home and talked Mum round, but only after she'd laid down the ground rules.

'You can wear your kit so long as you wash your hair and buy another pair of trainers, as the ones you insist on wearing look like a dog ate them, and we don't even own a dog.'

With Eddie's mum insisting he do the same, we'd agreed reluctantly; I couldn't bear to part with my lucky trainers. Not only had I made my highest score in them, I'd also taken a screamer catch. I wore them everywhere, but I didn't want to push my luck with Mum. And now, having just seen the players wearing their kit, I knew we'd totally made the right decision, although a tiny part of me really wished I was in my Australian kit.

We turned to watch the players continue to walk through the ground and into the big building farther along. With my heartbeat starting to return to normal, a man in a suit strode towards us. He introduced himself as Harvey Pointer. Dad seemed to know who he was as he shook hands with him. He was probably a similar age to my dad, but his face was weather-beaten from years of standing in the outfield sun, making him look much older. Judging by his height and broad shoulders, I thought he had to be a fast bowler, although his rounded belly meant he hadn't done too much bowling lately! I giggled as Eddie winked at me; he knew exactly what I'd been thinking.

Harvey turned to me, and I tried not to shy away. 'And you must be Tess, our competition winner?' Harvey said.

I stared at Harvey, willing some words to come out.

'Hi, I'm Eddie, Tess's best friend,' Eddie said, jumping in like he always did. For the millionth time I wished I could be more like Eddie. He always told me it didn't matter if I didn't talk too much: he thought I was one of the smartest people he knew, as I was always reading and writing things down. So, when I told him I'd entered the competition, he'd had absolutely no doubts that I would win. 'Tess is really happy to be here.'

Eddie and I met at cricket training four years ago, right after I'd moved to England from Australia. When some of the older kids had made fun of my accent and started bullying me, Eddie had stuck up for me, which I thought was really brave, as we were only eight at the time. Since then, we've been best friends. Although, we couldn't be any more different if we tried. Eddie had floppy blonde hair that was as messy and untidy as his clothes. I, on the other hand, had long black hair that I always had in neat braids, a tucked-in shirt and pulled-up socks. Still, we were best friends, and that was all that mattered. We loved batting together, as we always seemed to know what the other was thinking. And even though I had to take twice as many steps as Eddie's long legs, we had never, ever run each other out.

'Eddie, hi, pleased to meet you,' Harvey said, shaking his hand and giving me a smile. 'We're really happy to have you here, Tess. We all love your story and think it's incredible. And, of course, being in the middle of an Ashes series, it fits perfectly that you were born in Australia and are now living and playing cricket here. Nowadays, cricketers can play all around the world in so many different competitions. You summed it up perfectly saying that even though you can grow up and play for either country, right now all you want to do is play cricket because you love it. And that's what it should be about; all the rest will come later.'

Dad put his hand on my back, giving it a little rub, and I gave Harvey my best smile in reply, hoping he could see just how happy I was.

Harvey kept talking without missing a beat. 'And did you know your story is going to be printed in the programme for the Test?'

My mouth opened a little, but I closed it again. The fact that thousands of people would be reading my story made me feel even more anxious. Dad pressed a little harder and muttered, 'Manners.'

'Um, th-th-th-thank you,' I finally stammered, my cheeks burning.

'Well, I have a couple of copies for you to take home today as well, so you can read them tonight and make sure you bring them in tomorrow when you come back to watch the match.'

I turned to Eddie in time to see the disappointment cross his face before he flashed me a smile. We only had two tickets to the Test – for me and Dad. However, when Dad had explained to Harvey that Eddie and I were best friends and practically inseparable when it came to cricket, he'd been really nice, agreeing that Eddie could come along with us today.

'Shall we start our tour?' We followed Harvey as he explained he would take us to the Museum and then through the Pavilion. 'Unfortunately, the players' dressing rooms are off limits today as the players are already using them.'

Eddie and I exchanged a disappointed look. We'd really wanted to see the Honours Boards and sit in the seats of our favourite players.

Dad chatted to Harvey as we dawdled behind, checking everything out. Just before we came to the redbrick building the players had disappeared into, a gap appeared in between the stands, and I could see right across the ground to a funny spaceship-shaped building on the other side. Out in the middle, the England players in their light blue training kit were going through their training drills. Closest to us, a man rolled cricket balls on the grass for players to pick up and throw, trying to hit a single plastic stump in the ground.

'Look, Eddie, they're doing the exact same drills as we do!'

'Yeah, but a million times better,' Eddie replied, making me laugh as we watched ball after ball hit the single stump. We were lucky if even one ball hit, and we had three stumps to aim at!

A short round man marched towards Harvey, almost bowling us over. Eddie put out his hand to steady me before glaring at the man. He was puffing, and if his cheeks were any redder, I thought he could actually be mistaken for a cricket ball. He had the shiniest shoes I'd ever seen, dazzling me as the sun reflected off them. Harvey excused himself, almost kneeling in front of the man to correct the height difference as they talked.

I screwed up my nose. 'Who's that?'

'His name is Jasper Bardwell,' Eddie answered knowledgeably. 'He owns a bank. Dad says he's a multi-millionaire and one of the sponsors. See, his signs are all over the ground.'

As well as being our team coach, Eddie's Dad also had some kind of finance job. I looked around the ground and, sure enough, signs for 'Bardwell & Co.' were everywhere.

'Well, he gives me the creeps,' I whispered so that only Eddie could hear me. I turned back to watch the players train. Behind me, Dad took a deep breath and then whistled.

'Wowee, would you look at those stripes.'

I groaned. Dad loved cutting the grass and was totally obsessed about getting the perfect stripes, although the Lord's ones did look, and smell, pretty good.

I heard Harvey say my name and turned to see him pointing me out to Jasper Bardwell. Jasper Bardwell's top lip curled up in revulsion, making me feel like a piece of poo that would blemish his perfect shoes. I blushed as I turned away. What was his problem?

Harvey rejoined us. 'Sorry about that,' he said. His face was slightly flushed, and he rushed out his next words. 'That was Jasper Bardwell, one of our biggest sponsors. Tess, he wanted to meet you and congratulate you on your story but was running late for a meeting. Anyway, let's get on with the tour.'

Yeah, right, I thought, as I watched Jasper Bardwell's little legs and shiny shoes bounce away without a backward glance. I turned and did the same.

2

THE ASHES

Test series played between England and Australia Match

Harvey pointed out the Harris Gardens, where the biggest umbrellas I'd ever seen stretched out to protect the tables and chairs perfectly placed underneath them. A trellis wall of beautiful cream and pink-tinged clematis flowers caught my eye at the end of the Gardens. We passed under an archway and down a little alley wedged between two old four-storey buildings made from yellow brick. On our left was a shop selling cricket things.

Harvey stopped by the window.

'You can only shop in here if you are a member of the Marylebone or the Middlesex Cricket Clubs. In fact, all the buildings along here are for members' use only.' Harvey turned back to the shop window. 'The red and yellow colours, or egg and bacon as we like to call them, are for the MCC while the blue and pink are Middlesex.'

Farther along the alley was a doorway to the Real Tennis courts, which I knew was the game that Henry VIII used to play, as we'd seen his court when our school had visited Hampton Court Palace last year. It was different to the other tennis as it was played inside a small room, and the ball was allowed to bounce off the walls. What I didn't know was that Lord's had a court.

On our right was the back of the Pavilion. It had funny curved windows at ground level that I tried to peek through as we walked past; however, benches and pyramid-shaped trees blocked them, and I couldn't see anything exciting. We walked past an open doorway being guarded by an older man. His hair had gone grey and, even though he wasn't very tall, he stood very proudly in his blue jacket. He beamed as we passed and nodded his head in greeting. Eddie grinned back and gave him a little wave while I ducked my head before scolding myself for being so stupid.

After going under another arch, we turned left and stopped at the entrance to the Museum. Looking back at the Pavilion, I noticed that the bricks at the front were red while the ones at the back were yellow, and I wondered if this was where the egg and bacon colours came from.

'This is Alan,' Harvey said, pointing to the man behind the Museum desk. 'He's one of our stewards and will guide you through the Museum and answer any questions you might have. I'll meet you later and take you into the Pavilion.'

Dad murmured our thanks to Harvey as Alan clapped his hands in excitement, turning towards me. Just like the man guarding the Pavilion door, Alan was older and was grinning from ear to ear. They both obviously loved their jobs.

'I hear you're our very special guest today?' Alan said.

I nodded.

'Well, I can't wait to read your story tomorrow, I've heard it's very good.'

Dad gave me one of his looks, so I squeaked out a thank you. Alan reminded me a little of my grandpa, which helped me relax a tiny bit, but not enough to actually speak out loud. My grandpa was the coolest grandpa in the world, and also my hero. He loved cricket as much as me and he'd nearly cried when I told him I'd won the competition and was coming to Lord's. I knew he would love to work here like Alan, but he was now in a wheelchair after falling and breaking his hip a few years ago. He was the reason we'd moved to England, so Mum could help take care of him. Before we'd left this morning, Grandpa had slipped me £20 to buy something special from the gift shop. I tapped my pocket to make sure it was still there, and was reassured when I felt the bulge of the little purse it was in.

'I need to stay here until the security guard arrives, as it appears she's running a little late. It's her job to take the Urn over to the Pavilion later, so I'm sure she's making some last-minute security adjustments. We always hire an external company to help us transport the Urn when it's outside of its case - even if it's just from one room to another,' Alan said. 'In the meantime, why don't you wander about on the ground floor, then we can go upstairs to see the trophies – and please, ask me anything.'

Turning into the Museum, the first thing I noticed was a huge stained-glass window of a cricket match. Sunlight twinkled through the coloured glass like a rainbow onto the cricket-ball coloured carpet. Inside the Museum, glass cabinets crammed with everything and anything to do with cricket lined the walls. Dad spotted Shane Warne's green and gold shirt and moved towards it.

My eyes lit-up as Eddie and I walked as fast as we could, without running, to a room that had every kind of cricket game you could imagine. There were board games and card games and jigsaw puzzles, and so much more. Most of them looked really old.

'Look, Eddie, this is like the best ever.'

'I know, I really wish we could play them all.'

'Me too.'

'I don't think so, kids,' Dad said, coming up behind us

and crushing our dreams.

'It's not fair – we'd be really careful,' Eddie said.

Dad chuckled. 'I'm sure you would, but they must be special to be in here.'

Alan joined us and began to point out some of the games. 'I remember playing with some of these when I was just a lad.'

Eddie sighed. 'You're so lucky.'

Alan nodded. 'I certainly am. Follow me upstairs and I'll show you the Urn before it disappears.'

Reluctantly, Eddie and I left the games room and followed Alan and Dad up a very grand stone staircase. I trailed my hand up the golden handrail as I looked at all the cricket treasures. I couldn't believe my eyes as I came to the last step and saw that the grass-green carpet on the landing had been hoovered into stripes! I tugged Dad's shirt, pointed, and saw his little nod of appreciation.

Alan had stopped in front of two glass doors and I heard him tell Dad that behind them was an archive room. Not quite a library: there were no bookshelves, just wide drawers and storage boxes in the walls, but still someplace I'd like to look in one day.

'And here's the Urn,' Alan said.

Turning around, the Urn was in a glass box on top of a white stand. Dark red in colour, with two little teapot arms, it stood on a wooden base and seemed quite insignificant compared to the trophies in the cabinet next to it. I felt a little underwhelmed, wondering why everyone made such a fuss over it.

'It's really tiny for a trophy,' Eddie blurted out, also unimpressed, and Alan laughed.

'It is, I'm afraid. 10.5 centimetres high and it only weighs 124.8 grams. Although, you know it's not really a trophy, don't you?'

Eddie and I shook our heads, wondering what else it could be.

'Let me take you right back to when The Ashes began. It was 1882 and Australia had beaten England in a Test Match, in England, for the very first time. Of course, all Englishmen were mortified and the next day an obituary appeared in a newspaper declaring that English cricket had died, and that the ashes would be taken to Australia. Now, Ivo Bligh was the England captain at the time, and he vowed he would go to Australia and bring those ashes home. When England beat Australia, a lady called Florence Morphy presented Ivo with one of her perfume bottles and told him the ashes of a cricket bail were inside. On the front of the Urn, she stuck a little poem. Can you see what it says?'

Craning our necks forward, Eddie and I squinted, trying to read the writing. It was too small, and I couldn't make out any words. I shook my head while Eddie shrugged. 'I can't see anything,' he said.

'It says:

When Ivo goes back with the urn, the urn;
Studds, Steel, Read and Tylecote return, return;
The welkin will ring loud;
The great crowd will feel proud;
Seeing Barlow and Bates with the urn, the urn;
And the rest coming home with the urn.'

Eddie glanced at me – I had no idea what it meant either.

Alan smiled at our confused faces. 'It's a poem that was published in a magazine in Melbourne. What it means is that everyone at home in England would be proud when Ivo and his team returned home as winners and cricket was rightly returned to England. Do you know what happened next?'

Eddie and I shook our heads.

'Ivo Bligh and Florence Morphy fell in love. Ivo had to return to England after the series, but he went back to Australia as soon as he could, and they married in 1884. Florence moved to England, and they lived at Cobham Hall, where the Urn stayed on the mantelpiece in the library until Ivo died in 1927, then Florence donated it to the MCC.'

Wow, no wonder it was so special. It was as good as any fairy tale, I thought, while Eddie just rolled his eyes. I poked my tongue out at him and he rolled his eyes again, this time with a huge grin.

'Are there really ashes inside it?' Eddie asked,

changing the subject.

'That's a very good question. We've had it scanned and there certainly are ashes or residue inside. What it is, we don't know because it's never been opened. Even when it was sent away to have some cracks repaired, the company was given strict instructions not to remove the cork. And that's part of the mystery.'

'And it stays here, even if Australia wins the series?' Dad asked with a smirk.

Alan gave him a knowing smile back before answering. 'Yes, it stays here. As I said, the Urn has never been used as an actual trophy, it is simply symbolic of the relationship between the two countries. A glass trophy in the shape of an urn was made in 1998 for the winning team to keep. Although, having said all that, the Urn has travelled to Australia on a few occasions; however, we don't like to take it out of this cabinet too many times as it's very fragile, and irreplaceable.'

'That's really cool,' Eddie said.

'And that's the story of The Ashes,' Alan concluded. 'Oh, I almost forgot. As I said, the Urn is being taken over to the Long Room shortly, as the two captains are having their photo taken with it today, so you might be lucky and get to see it out of its case.'

Eddie and I exchanged an excited look. 'I can't wait to see it up close,' I whispered to him as we left the trophies behind and walked along the landing. 'But what's the Long Room?'

'I don't know,' Eddie replied. 'But if that's where the Urn's going to be, then I want to be there too.'

Below us, someone was shouting. Eddie and I peered over the railing in time to see a man with a huge camera around his neck being shoved out of the Museum's reception area by a female security guard. Dressed in all black clothing with reddish hair, she was a lot younger than the stewards I'd seen, and steadier on her feet, so I could understand why they'd hired a security company to transport the Urn to the Long Room. Hearing how fragile it was, I know I'd be too nervous to touch it, let alone carry it anywhere.

'I have a right to be here, you can't throw me out,' the man shouted.

'You've been told you before, you're not allowed back. Now leave,' the lady replied. She sounded annoyed, as if she had somewhere else to be.

'You can't do this. You can't treat me this way. Let me go or I'll make you pay.'

Dad tugged at my arm to come away. I felt really bad for the lady. The man was in her face, yelling at her. I knew what it was like to be bullied, and it wasn't right that he was treating her that way. I felt a wave of anger rise inside me. I wanted to stand up and say something for her and other people who were bullied. But, as usual, I shied away, too scared to make a fuss.

'Leave it, kids, it's nothing to do with us,' Dad said, pulling us both away.

'My apologies,' Alan said with a little frown. 'That man has been at Lord's all week. We think he's a journalist looking for a story; however, he keeps changing his own story as to why he's here. We're not sure how he's getting back in, nor what he wants. Anyway, not to worry, the security guard is taking care of it. Come along.'

I risked one more peek over the railing to see the security guard push the man again. The man recoiled from her as if he'd smelled something rotten. He threw her a look of revulsion before striding off. The lady looked really stressed and began muttering to herself: 'I don't need this, today of all days. Focus, just focus on what you need to do.'

The whole thing was really bizarre. She obviously had enough to worry about today without some pesky reporter getting in her face. Reluctantly, I followed everyone through a doorway to where Harvey was waiting in a corridor. Maybe my bravery would come another day. Behind Harvey was a small staircase and a sign pointing to the Library, which I hoped would be our next stop.

'This concludes my part of your tour,' Alan said as he shook everyone's hands. 'Harvey will now take you into the Pavilion. Enjoy the rest of your day, and, Tess, congratulations again on your story.'

As disappointed as I was that we weren't going into the Library, I couldn't help but giggle when I saw Eddie's relieved face. He hated reading almost as much as I loved it. I could totally understand why, as he had a photographic memory. The more he read, the more information got clogged in his brain, so he chose to read only what he had to.

3

TOUR

When your team travels away from their home ground to play a number of matches

Crossing over a little walkway, Harvey held open a heavy double door and suddenly we were in the Pavilion. But it was nothing like our club pavilion. It was like one of those massive old houses that Mum dragged me to every summer. However, instead of the stuffy portraits and paintings of horses and dogs, the pale walls were covered in paintings and photographs of cricket players and cricket grounds. And even though I didn't recognise many of the faces, Dad obviously did, by the sparkle in his eyes. The staircase was even grander than the one in the Museum, with ornate iron spindles which, to my astonishment, bore the letters 'MCC', like on the Grace Gates. It was all so beautiful, and Mum would have loved it. I wanted to take some photos so I could show her, but was too scared to ask. I jabbed Eddie in the side and pointed to my phone. He immediately understood and nodded.

'Harvey, can we take photos in here?'

'I'm afraid not.'

'Okay, no worries.' Eddie turned to me and shrugged. I shoved my phone in my pocket so I wouldn't be tempted.

'As I said, unfortunately we can't go into the players' dressing rooms, so I'll show you a few other special rooms before we go to the Long Room and meet the captains.' My stomach did a tiny flip. Eddie flashed me a quick smile and my stomach calmed a little, knowing he'd be right there with me.

Going down the staircase, Harvey turned into a blue room that overlooked the ground. 'This is the Bowlers Bar. Do you know why it's called that?'

'Because only bowlers are allowed in here?' Eddie said.

'Good guess, and you're almost right. Originally, the men playing for England came from different social classes. The Amateurs, or Gentlemen, were from the upper and middle classes, while the Professionals came from the working class. Gentlemen were always the captains, and for the most part they were batsmen, as they thought bowling was too hard work. They treated the Professionals like servants, making them stay in separate hotels and use separate changing rooms. So, the room below us was where the Professionals, or bowlers, had their changing room.'

'That's like at the Sydney Cricket Ground,' Dad said. 'When it was being built, the MCC requested that the away dressing room be split into two levels. The Gentlemen sat on the top level and the Professionals below.'

'That's really mean,' I said in a voice barely above a whisper.

Harvey heard me and I blushed. 'It is, but you have to remember it was a different time back then.' He quickly moved the conversation on. 'Can you see the bell hanging from the balcony? That's the Five-Minute Bell, which is rung every morning of a match to signal that it's nearly time to start playing. Recently, the MCC began inviting people to ring the bell for Test Matches, and it's become one of the MCC's most honoured traditions. You have to be very special to be asked – I haven't been, yet! Come on, there's lots more to see.'

Going back up the staircase to the second floor, Harvey led us down a corridor that ran the length of the Pavilion, pointing out the gym and some function rooms before we came to the grand staircase, only it wasn't the same one we'd used before: this had totally different cricketers and cricket grounds in the paintings. I couldn't quite believe the Pavilion had not one but two grand staircases. We followed Harvey into the Players' Dining Room. It was a small room with three tables set up ready for tomorrow's hungry cricketers. Through a doorway was the kitchen, where a number of chefs were preparing food.

'All the players, umpires and officials sit together to have their tea,' Harvey said.

'Just like our club room,' I whispered to Eddie.

'Yep, but I bet they don't serve up dodgy egg sandwiches,' Eddie whispered back. I laughed at Eddie's joke and took a deep breath in. The smells wafting from the kitchen were amazing, and definitely not egg sandwiches.

'It's quite small,' Dad said.

'Yes,' Harvey agreed. 'Originally, teams only had about thirteen players and officials, so everyone fitted comfortably. Nowadays, squads can have over thirty players; plus, there's umpires, officials, scorers, physios, etc., so it can get crowded.'

Crowded! I didn't even think the room was big enough for our U13s team, let alone all the England and Australian players AND the umpires.

Harvey pointed to a sideboard in the kitchen. 'We always have a replica Urn on display during The Ashes so the players, and chefs, don't forget what's at stake.'

Two men wearing chef uniforms came bustling into the room, speaking at one hundred miles an hour.

'I told you last week there was none left,' the first man said.

'And I told you to order some more,' the other man replied.

'And I did, it just might not arrive today. Does it really matter? It's only ice cream.'

The second man, clearly the Head Chef, rounded on the other man, jabbing a finger in his face. 'It might just be ice cream to you, but to me it's my reputation. I ALWAYS do the best lunch, and nothing and no one will stop me from doing that.'

Rebuked, the first man began to retreat out of the dining room. 'I'll chase it up right now.'

'You better, 'cause if it's not here before the end of the day you'll either be looking for a new job or you'll have to find a way to delay the start of the –'

The Head Chef stopped mid-sentence when he saw us staring. He frowned then broke into a smile, suddenly full of charm. 'Welcome, welcome. I'm sorry you had to hear all that. Who have we got here?'

'Geoff, this is Tess, her father, Mitch, and Eddie. Tess is our competition winner.' Harvey had already begun herding us out of the room as he replied.

'Congrats; well, I won't get in your way,' Geoff said, clearly wanting us to leave.

'Sorry about that,' Harvey said as we left the room. 'You can understand how stressed everyone is the day before a Test. It might seem strange to get upset about not having enough ice cream, but it's the most popular item on the menu. I'm sure everything is under control.'

I leaned in close to make some quip about ice cream to Eddie. Dad caught my eye and shook his head, so I leaned back. Eddie just grinned: he knew exactly what I was going to say.

In the Committee Room, Harvey showed us where the King and Queen sat whenever they came to the cricket. 'They don't have to queue like everyone else. Instead, their car drives all the way to the Pavilion doors and they walk straight up the staircase and into this room.'

Next, Harvey pointed out the England and Australia dressing rooms and took us out onto the balcony to look over the ground. He pointed out all the stands, telling us who each one was named after and when they were built.

'The Media Stand has become an iconic building since it was completed in 1999, just in time for the men's World Cup that year. Behind that, you can see the Nursery Ground, which is used for training and some matches, and to the right is our Indoor Cricket Academy.'

Dad asked a bunch of boring questions, so Eddie and I watched the groundsmen scurrying on the grass like little ants. Eddie began turning his head left and right.

'Is it just me or does the ground really slope to the right?'

'It's not you,' Harvey said. 'It's about an eight-foot slope.'

'Wow, that's pretty big,' Eddie said.

'It is, so seam bowlers like to bowl from this end, the Pavilion End, while swing bowlers bowl from the Nursery End to get the ball to swing away from the batters and down the slope. Which end would you two bowl from?'

'So, I'd be from the Nursery End, as I'm good at swinging it, and Tess is a leggie, so she'd bowl from the Pavilion End and spin it up the slope.'

'Sounds like you two make the perfect bowling partnership,' Harvey said, smiling. 'I hope I'll never have to face you.'

Eddie and I beamed. I really hoped we'd both get to play here one day.

'Can you see the weathervane above the clock?' Harvey said. Eddie and I nodded; it was the same one I'd seen when we'd arrived. 'Well, it's called Father Time and some people think he's putting the bails on to start the day, while others believe he's taking them off the stumps at the end of the day. What do you think?'

'Putting them on, I think,' Eddie said, and I nodded in agreement. ''Cause everyone comes here to watch cricket and you see him as soon as you get here, so you know it's nearly time to start the game.'

'Hmm, that makes sense,' Harvey agreed. 'Right, that's nearly all of the tour for now. You can take a few photos here if you like before we head back inside.'

Eddie and I grabbed our phones and took a few selfies, and Dad made me get a photo with him before Harvey took one of all of us. Harvey's walkie-talkie crackled into life and he listened intently before smiling.

'The Urn's on its way. Let's get a good spot so we have the best view.'

4

DROPPED A SITTER
When a fielder drops an easy catch

Eddie and I stood in front of the door to the Long Room. Even though I could only get a glimpse, it looked as grand as a ballroom, with its high carved ceiling and chandeliers. Stewards lined the staircase while a few other people stood behind them waiting. The door to the Australian dressing room opened on the floor above and the Australian and England captains came out, chatting with each other. Eddie nudged me and we both gawped.

Still holding my phone, I slid it into camera mode; there was no way I was going to miss getting a photo of the two captains. I raised it and watched them descend the stairs, waiting for the perfect moment.

The captains reached the bottom of the stairs and turned towards the Long Room. I only had one chance and needed to take it. Lifting my phone even higher, I moved my finger ready to press the button. There was a hush as the security guard we'd seen arguing with the man this morning entered the Pavilion carrying the Urn. She looked really nervous, and who would blame her? I'd be petrified to touch something so precious.

'Tess,' Harvey whispered, tapping me urgently on the shoulder. 'You can't take photos in here, remember?'

Everyone stared at me, even the two captains, and I felt my face grow redder than a brand-new cricket ball. I quickly dropped my shaking hands. As I did, my finger hit the button and the flash went off, right into the eyes of the security guard carrying the Urn. She stumbled, and despite desperately trying to steady herself, tripped again. Her legs wobbled as she began to fall towards the floor.

As she crashed, her elbows hit the ground, causing the Urn to fly up into the air. Everyone gasped, but all I could think about was Dad's favourite story of Herschelle Gibbs dropping an easy catch, and Steve Waugh telling him he'd dropped the World Cup. This was just like that, only a million times worse.

The Urn did a spectacular somersault in the air before

falling to the floor, landing on the top step. It bounced and flipped, landing on the step below, and continued its somersault dance down the staircase until it landed with a *plop* at the bottom. I looked up. Everyone had the same look of horror etched on their face.

Nobody moved, nobody breathed, and then, all at once, chaos broke out as everyone rushed forward. I was gasping for breath as people pushed and shoved forward, craning their necks to see the fate of the Urn. I couldn't move. I couldn't breathe. I couldn't believe what I'd just done. Somebody shoved my shoulder, pushing me backwards before stepping on my foot. It really hurt and I grabbed my foot, hopping madly on the other one. The pain was a welcome distraction from how much trouble I was in.

'Tess, Eddie, come with me,' Harvey shouted above the noise. A tightness spread across my chest as I hopped-walked up the stairs. At the top, I tried to peer over to see how badly the Urn was broken, but Dad shoved me along. Although, it didn't matter: even the tiniest crack was bad enough. For a moment, I thought Harvey was taking us into the Australian dressing room. Instead, he kept walking down a narrow corridor and through a door. I was almost hyperventilating as Harvey slumped against the door, rubbing his hands over his face.

'This is my office. Stay here while I find out what's going to happen next,' he said before slamming the door behind him.

Dad turned to me and snatched away my phone. It was all I deserved. He was seething and had the angriest face I'd ever seen, and I gulped back tears. I was in so much trouble. Not that I needed him to tell me that. Of course I was in trouble. Ten minutes ago I'd been having the best day of my life, even better than when I'd hit the winning runs in last year's final. And now I felt awful, horrible, worse than being bowled middle stump for a golden duck.

Dad gritted his teeth, trying to remain calm when I knew he was ready to explode. 'What were you thinking? You were told not to take photos.'

'I know, I'm sorry, Dad. I didn't mean to.'

'Of course you didn't mean to. But that doesn't make it any better. You didn't listen and now you've ruined the whole day. You're just lucky the Urn didn't break, otherwise you would have ruined cricket as well.'

I felt sick in my stomach and turned my head away so that no one could see my tears. Dad turned away too. I could almost hear the steam blowing out of his nose as he tried to control his temper. I couldn't bear to look at him.

'But that's the thing,' Eddie said in a quiet voice. 'If it's as old and fragile as everyone says, why didn't it break?'

5

STICKY WICKET

A wet and soft pitch that makes the ball hard to play

Before we could think about what Eddie had said, Harvey burst through the door with such gusto that the draught ruffled the papers on his desk. Eddie reached out to steady them.

'I need to speak to you right away,' he said, gesturing for Dad to follow him. 'We also need your phone, Tess.'

I stood up, ready to face Harvey. An apology formed in my head, but as usual the words twisted and turned and got stuck in my throat. All I could do was drop my head in shame while Dad handed over my phone. Eddie spoke up for me instead. 'Tess is really sorry; she really didn't mean for all of this to happen.'

Harvey looked confused, rather than angry. Or maybe he was just as shocked as the rest of us and didn't know what to do next. 'I know, and I appreciate you saying so, but right now I need you two to stay here while we sort this mess out.' He turned back to the door and let Dad pass before he closed it behind him.

I collapsed into the nearest chair, grabbed one of my plaits and used it to wipe my tears before flapping it against my forehead. If I hit my head hard enough, maybe it would erase the last ten minutes from my memory. 'Thanks, Eddie, but you don't need to stick up for me, I know I'm in heaps of trouble.'

'Didn't you hear what I said before?' I shrugged and Eddie continued. 'The Urn didn't break. Why?'

'What do you mean, "why"?' The stupid stairs are probably soft so people walking up and down them don't hurt their feet.'

'Yeah, maybe if it only hit one step, but it bounced all the way to the bottom. It's like over 100 years old and is really fragile. It should have broken.'

I rolled my eyes. What on earth was Eddie on about? I just wanted him to stop talking, but he couldn't let it go.

'So, I think it didn't break because it's not real.'

'Not real? That doesn't make any sense. I know you're

trying to make me feel better, but it doesn't matter. None of this would have happened if it wasn't for me. It's all my fault.'

'It's not your fault – well, maybe; but just listen to me.' Eddie walked closer to me then grabbed his nose. 'Geez, Tess, you stink.'

'Hey!' I knew I was in trouble, but it wasn't like Eddie to be so mean.

'No, really, you smell. Did you stand in something?'

I sighed and buried my face in my plaits. Life really sucked right now. Then a putrid smell wafted into my nostrils, making me gag. I grabbed my nose. 'Urgh, I do stink. What *is* that?'

Twisting my feet left and right I tried to see if anything was on them. There, on the outside of my brand-new left trainer was a dark patch that hadn't been there this morning. Mum was going to flip. If only I'd been wearing my lucky trainers, then none of this would have happened. It couldn't have been there long, otherwise we would have smelt it before.

'It smells like rat poo,' Eddie said, and I gave him a wry smile. Eddie's horrid big brother had pushed him into a pile of rat poo at their grandparents' farm last summer, so he would know exactly what it smelled like.

'Eew! I've got to get it off.' I reached for my pocket. Mum always made me carry a packet of tissues.

'Those tissues won't be enough,' Eddie said as I gagged again. 'Let's go find a toilet.'

'But we're supposed to stay here,' I replied.

'Well, you can stay here if you like, but give me your shoe and I'll go clean it before we both throw up.'

Eddie reached his hand towards me. I couldn't let him do that for me, he'd already done more than enough. I sighed. 'No, it's okay. I'll go. Do you remember where they were?'

'Of course,' Eddie said, grinning.

The crowd of people had dispersed when we emerged, and the Urn had been removed from the bottom of the staircase. Even so, we kept as far away from the stairs as possible as we dashed across the landing and through the opposite door. We ran down the corridor to the Ladies toilet. Eddie held the door open for me so I went in assuming he would follow. Instead, he hesitated, and I groaned.

'Geez, Eddie, don't be stupid. Are you going to wait out here and risk someone seeing you, or just suck it up and come inside?' Eddie hesitated a fraction longer before following me. While I grabbed some paper towels and tried to clean my shoe, Eddie gazed out the window. 'What are you looking at?'

'I don't know, it's really weird. Everyone's disappeared. It was so busy when we first got here.'

'That is really weird. Urgh! That was gross. I think I got it all.' I threw the dirty paper into the bin and washed my hands. I was barely listening to Eddie. Even though the poo was gone, my chest still felt tight, reminding me what I'd done. 'Let's go back to Harvey's office before we get in even more trouble.'

'Wait a minute,' Eddie said, and I paused mid-step. 'I really think there's something off with the Urn.'

I sighed. 'Come on, Eddie, give it a rest.'

'Just listen, okay?'

'Fine!' I really wasn't in the mood to listen to Eddie's conspiracy theory.

'If it had been the real Urn that the security guard was carrying, it would have broken when it hit the floor. But it didn't, so I think it must be a fake. And now, there's no one about so I think everyone's been herded into one area until the police arrive so they can question them.'

'I don't know, Eddie. It all sounds a bit far-fetched for me. I mean, how would anyone even steal the Urn? It's kept under strict lock and key. And when would they have had the opportunity?'

'I don't know either. So, maybe the question should be how long has a fake one been inside the Museum, and whether anyone would have noticed during the photoshoot today if the security guard hadn't dropped it?'

I was about to tell Eddie he was mad when a thought crossed my mind. 'Eddie, I think you're right! Remember how everyone rushed forwards to see where the Urn landed? Well, when someone stood on my foot it was because they were pushing past me, away from the Urn.'

Eddie's face lit up. 'Because they knew the Urn wouldn't break.'

'Exactly, and why would they know that?'

'Because they were the one who swapped it in the first place. Yes, I knew I was right. Is that the same foot that had rat poo on it?'

'Oh my goodness, it is!'

'Then that's our first clue! They must have stood in rat poo and transferred it to your shoe when they stood on you. But who was it? Did you get a good look at them?'

I frowned, trying to remember. It was all such a rush and the only thing I could remember was seeing the Urn doing somersaults in the air and bouncing down the stairs. I shook my head to clear that memory, hopefully forever.

'No, I didn't. I was too worried about the fact it was all my fault, and then my foot was hurting.' It suddenly dawned on me that it wasn't the real Urn I'd made the security guard drop. The tightness in my chest suddenly didn't feel so tight. I could never have lived with myself if I'd broken the real one and totally ruined cricket.

'Dang it! We have to try and work out who was missing when the Urn hit the bottom of the steps, and where they went,' Eddie said, his face glowing with excitement.

'But who would want to steal the Urn?' I asked.

6

TARGET

The number of runs the team batting last must score to win a match

'It has to be someone who had access to the Museum,' Eddie said. 'Hey, what about that journalist at the Museum? Alan said he'd been hanging around and acting all suspicious. It would make a good story, especially if he suddenly shows up with the real Urn and takes all the credit for finding it.'

'Could be ... He was making a big fuss, though. If I

was going to steal something, not that I ever would, but if I was, I'd be trying not to draw attention to myself.'

'That makes sense, but it's still not worth ruling him out,' Eddie agreed reluctantly.

'Or how about the chef – what was his name? Oh, Geoff?' I said.

Eddie rolled his eyes. 'I doubt that not having ice cream is enough to make someone steal the Urn?'

'Fine,' I replied, a little put out that Eddie had dismissed my idea so easily. I still didn't understand why anyone would want to steal the Urn. But I also didn't want Eddie to be the only one who was allowed to come up with suggestions. 'Only he was so mad and threatened the other man. The Urn going missing might buy him some time? Oh, there was a replica Urn in the kitchen, remember? So, he could easily have used that to swap the original.'

'Oh yeah, that's right,' Eddie said, and I gave myself a little smile of satisfaction. 'But how would he get rat poo on his foot? His kitchen must be really clean?'

'I don't know … Maybe in a storage room or something?'

Eddie leaned against the wall. 'Hmm, how about we go to the kitchen and see if the replica Urn is still there, and check if there are any other clues? If we find anything smelly, we might be on to something.'

'Maybe we should tell Dad and Harvey and see what they think?' It was all starting to get a little out of control.

It was one thing to think the Urn might actually be stolen, and another to go running around Lord's looking for it. And even if it wasn't the real Urn that had dropped onto the floor, I was still in a heap of trouble and I knew that the longer we stayed away, the more trouble we'd be in.

'As if they're going to believe us. Let's just search the Dining Room and kitchen first and then go back to Harvey's office. No one will miss us before then, and if they do, we'll just say we went to the toilet. Come on, we can be proper detectives. Like Sherlock Holmes.'

It was a low blow and Eddie knew it. I couldn't resist anything to do with Sherlock Holmes. Already halfway to the door, he stopped dead in his tracks as his mind-computer whirred into action. He held one finger in the air, looking very matter of fact. 'I bet you didn't know that Arthur Conan Doyle played cricket? And you'll never guess who he played against. W.G. Grace, that's who, and not only that, he also took W.G. Grace's wicket.'

'You're joking, right?' It never ceased to amaze me how many random facts Eddie had in his super-brain. 'That's so cool!'

'Yep, so we can be proper cricket detectives, just like him.'

Grinning, I followed Eddie out of the toilets. As we entered the Dining Room, we could hear a voice coming from the kitchen. Eddie pointed to a nearby table. We ducked under it, pulling the tablecloth down, leaving a little gap to peer through. I spied half-cooked food in pots,

and ingredients lying half-cut on chopping boards. It was obvious that everyone had left in a hurry, except for one man, who was on his phone. I pulled the tablecloth open just a fraction more and could almost see the spot where the Urn had been. The man turned around and looked in our direction. I shrank back, hoping he hadn't seen me. But I'd seen him.

'It's Geoff,' I whispered to Eddie. He nodded and held his finger in front of his mouth to shush me. My eyes grew rounder and rounder as I listened to him speak.

'Yes, I've got it … It's all gone to plan in the end – well, mostly … No, it's all good, nobody else knows … I'm leaving now and will meet you there …'

Geoff hung up his phone then stuffed something in his pocket before striding out of the kitchen. However, instead of going out the Dining Room door, he walked to the far corner of the room and opened what appeared to be a cupboard. Inside was a dumb waiter, used to carry food up and down. He climbed inside, hit the button, and disappeared.

Eddie scrambled out from under the table and started jumping around excitedly. 'Did you see that? He escaped down the dumb waiter. That was so cool.'

'I know, right? It's like the perfect getaway. And did you hear him? He literally admitted he'd stolen the Urn.' Excitement started to bubble in my belly as I realised that we might actually be on to something.

'It's the perfect crime, Eddie said. 'Tess, we're

geniuses!'

I beamed with pride. Eddie and I really were geniuses; we were the only ones who had figured it all out. That meant we were the only ones who could solve the case and catch the thief.

'Come on, we have to follow him.' Eddie rushed to the dumb waiter and impatiently hit the button, waiting for the lift to return to our level. It was a small space, but if Geoff was able to fit in, then we must be able to as well.

'You go first,' I said to Eddie. He curled up his long legs and shoved as far back as he could go. Climbing in, I managed to squeeze into the remaining space before pressing the button. It was the slowest lift in the world, taking forever until it finally juddered to a halt and the door slid open. The dumb waiter had landed outside, opposite the Pavilion. There was no sign of Geoff or, luckily, the steward who had been guarding the Pavilion doors, which were now securely locked. It was so eerily quiet inside the Lord's walls, yet beyond them I could hear the hum of London life going about its business, not realising the theft of the century had just taken place.

'Where's he gone?' I whispered?

'I dunno,' Eddie replied as he crawled out of the cramped space. He looked left and right while I uncurled my squished legs and slid out. 'He must have gone this way.'

Eddie pointed around the corner to where the Museum was and strode off. Beyond the Museum was a small car park. Crouching behind a car, we could see Geoff talking to a man guarding the gate. We couldn't hear exactly what they were saying, but by the way Geoff was flapping his arms about it was obvious he wanted to open the gates. Only the security guard wasn't budging. After a few minutes of arguing, he held up his hand to Geoff and began to talk into his walkie-talkie. Geoff paced back and forth and kept looking at his watch. Before long, his patience wore out and when the security guard turned his back, he pounced on the gates and began unlocking them.

'He's getting away.' Eddie rose to run after him, but I dragged him back down. A delivery van turned and drove through the gates, coming to a stop not far from where we were hiding. We crouched down further, keeping one eye on Geoff in case he made a run for it through the open gate. Instead, he remonstrated with the security guard once more before striding towards the van.

'Thanks, mate, you've saved my life,' Geoff said as he signed for the delivery and clapped his hands together. The delivery driver unlocked the van doors to reveal boxes of ice cream. Geoff pulled a scrunched-up wad of papers from his pocket and ticked off the boxes as they were unloaded.

'Sorry we didn't have any chocolate,' the delivery driver said as he unloaded the last box.

'It's all good. I'm just grateful I have any ice cream, as it was looking like we'd have nothing this morning. I'll make do with what you've got, and no one will be the wiser.'

I sighed. There was no mystery here, and Geoff most definitely wasn't our thief. He must have been talking to the ice cream delivery driver when we heard him on the phone and not plotting to steal the Urn. In fact, he couldn't stop beaming as he pushed the trolley of ice cream back to the Pavilion. His crisis was over, and we could strike him off our list of suspects.

'I was certain he was trying to escape with the Urn,' Eddie said, slumping against the car.

'Me too, but at least now there's ice cream.'

'Huh! I mean, how could we possibly think it was him? If he wanted to buy some extra time, I'm sure there were plenty of ways to cause a commotion. Besides, the Urn was replaced with a fake, so the thief wasn't expecting to be caught. I guess we danced down the wicket too early.'

'Yeah, and we got stumped,' I said, and Eddie gave me a grim smile. 'So, where does that leave us? We can't just keep pointing fingers at people accusing them of stealing the Urn when we have no actual proof.'

'Except for the rat poo,' Eddie replied.

'How do we even know if it's connected if we don't know where it came from?'

'It has to be. It only appeared on your foot when someone pushed past you AFTER the Urn was dropped.'

'So, the thief has to be the one who stood on my foot?'

'Exactly'.

'So, we just have to work out where the rat poo could

have come from.'

Eddie's face was a mask of concentration as his brain scrolled through his memories. 'Hey, I know! There are some old train tunnels that run under Lord's. There would definitely be rat poo in them.'

'And that would also be a great way to get in and out of the ground without being seen. Do you know where the entrance is?'

'Nope,' Eddie said.

'Dang it! Oh, but I reckon there might be some plans or a book or something in the Library that might tell us where it is.'

Eddie twitched at the idea he might have to go into a library. I knew he was about to argue with me when the wail of approaching Police sirens drowned him out. 'They have to be coming here,' he shouted, then sighed. 'Come on, I guess the dreaded Library is where we have to go, and quickly, before the police arrive.'

'How are we going to get back in? Geoff will have used the dumb waiter to get the ice cream up to the kitchen.'

'We're going to use this,' Eddie replied, taking a security card out of his pocket.

I gasped. 'Where did you get that?'

'From Harvey's desk.'

'You stole it?'

'No, I borrowed it. I thought we'd need it to get back to his office after we went to the toilets. I didn't think we'd be away this long, though. I'm going to give it back.'

'You better!'

'I will, I promise. Now, let's go.'

We snuck back into the Pavilion and across the little walkway to the Library, just as the police cars pulled through the Grace Gates.

7

REVERSE SWING

When the bowler gets the ball to move in the opposite direction to what the batter is expecting

'Who knew there were so many books about cricket,' I said, breathing in the beautiful smell of paper and leather. I looked around the Library, taking in the shelves upon shelves of books, reading desks and sofas across the two levels. Eddie gave me a shrug then climbed the stairs to the upper level. I smiled as I watched him out of the corner of my eye. He was trying to make it look like he was inspecting the bookshelves; instead, he was actually looking out of the window.

I ran my finger across the book spines, hoping something inspirational would jump out at me. I would have loved nothing more than to pull each and every book from the shelves, snuggle on the sofa and read them from cover to cover. My fingers touched a book that was just what we were looking for. Grateful that I hadn't used my tissues to clean my shoe, I grabbed one from my pocket and wrapped it around the spine before removing the book from the shelf, just in case the thief had touched the book before me. I wouldn't want to smudge their fingerprints.

'Have you found anything that will help?' Eddie asked.

I nodded. 'This book's called *50 Facts about Lord's You Didn't Know*. I bet it has something that can help us.'

'Sounds good,' Eddie replied. 'I'll keep an eye out of the window and you read that. Shout out if there's anything useful and I'll come and memorise it.'

'I will not "shout out",' I scolded. 'We're in a library!'

'Okay, fine,' Eddie moaned. 'Speak in a volume suitable for a library when you find something interesting.'

Giggling, I flopped onto the couch; it really was as snuggly as it looked, and it didn't take long for me to become engrossed. The book had some really cool facts. Like, the first Pavilion had burned down in 1825 and the new one was opened in 1890. And the Nursery Ground literally used to be an actual nursery before the MCC bought it!

'Oh, Dad will love this one,' I whispered loudly to Eddie. 'It says the first lawnmower was bought in 1864. Before that they used sheep to keep the grass down.'

'That's really cool, Tess, but it doesn't help us find out if there's an entrance to the tunnels, and we're in a bit of a hurry.' Eddie tapped on his watch as if to prove the point.

'I guess not.' I sighed, closing the book. Something caught my eye, and I hastily reopened it. My eyes widened as I read it. This was exactly what we were after.

'The police have gone into the Pavilion,' Eddie said, still staring out of the window. 'There's lots –' He froze mid-sentence and grabbed hold of the windowsill.

'What is it? You're supposed to be looking for clues.'

'It's the journalist from this morning, the one making a big fuss outside the Museum.'

'What?' I walked, not ran, as you should never run in a library, as quickly as I could to join him. Sure enough, there he was, sneaking around under the stands. 'Why isn't he with everyone else?'

'I dunno. He's already on our suspect list and now he's looking even more suspicious.'

We watched him dart in and out of our view as he hid behind the giant pillars. He paused before looking up to our window as if he knew we were there. Gasping, we dropped to the floor.

'Do you think he saw us?' I whispered.

'I don't think so … I sure hope not,' Eddie whispered back. 'I'll take another look.'

Slowly, Eddie pushed himself up onto his knees and peered out the window. 'I can't see him anymore, but there are police everywhere.'

'How do you think he knew we were here?'

'I'm not sure. He's definitely shifty, though. We need to find the entrance to the tunnels and fast.

'Uh-oh,' Eddie added as he sank to floor once more.

'What?'

'Your dad's seen me.'

'WHAT?!?' I screeched, totally forgetting I was in a library. 'How?'

'We're opposite Harvey's office and he's looking out the window straight at us.'

Eddie's phone buzzed in his pocket.

'Is that my dad? Are you going to answer it?'

'I dunno.'

The phone rang out. Then immediately started ringing again. Eddie turned it off and shoved it in his pocket.

'We're in so much trouble,' I said. Eddie risked a peek out of the window. 'Is he still there?'

'No.'

'So, he's on his way here?'

'I dunno.'

'Eddie! What are we going to do?'

'I dunno.'

'Stop saying that. We need a plan.'

'Okay, fine. What do you want to do? We can stay here and face your dad and the consequences, or keep going with our search for the stolen Urn?

I stuck my plait in my mouth and thought hard. One part of me really wanted to keep going with our investigation. As far as I knew, we were the only ones who knew the Urn had been stolen and replaced with a fake. And we were the only ones who had any clues. Would my dad and the police believe us if we told them? Probably not. The other part of me was saying this was a matter for grown-ups. We were just kids, what did we know about finding a thief? It was scary and dangerous, and we really should be letting the police handle it. But we had found the clues.

'Well?' Eddie said, tapping his foot impatiently.

'Well, what do you think?'

'I think that we've gone this far so we might as well keep going?'

'But Dad's going to be so angry with us.'

Eddie shrugged. 'He's angry with us anyway. And he's probably on his way here right now. Have you found anything in that book that tells us where the tunnels are? If so, then let's go. If not, then let's face the music.'

I looked down at the book I was holding, remembering what I'd just read. I had definitely found something that would help us find the tunnels. I chewed on my plait one last time. Eddie was right: Dad was going to be angry one way or another.

I opened my mouth to give Eddie the good news but froze as the Library door handle started to rattle.

Eddie grabbed my hand and dragged me behind a bookshelf that separated the two floors. The door creaked opened and we held our breath, waiting for Dad to shout out our names. But he didn't. Maybe it wasn't him? But who else could it be? Gripping hold of Eddie's arms to steady me, I leaned out, hoping to get a glimpse of the person. I had caught Eddie off guard and he stepped back to regain his balance. I heard a *click* as his foot stood on something. We both looked down. Eddie's foot was twisted at an awkward angle and rested on top of a button. What on earth could it be for?

Stay still, I thought as I stared directly at Eddie's face. He gave me the slightest of nods, petrified to move. We could hear the person rifling through the drawers of the desk and pulling books off the bookshelves. It would only be a matter of seconds before they came up to our level and found us in our absolutely rubbish hiding spot. Sweat began to bead on Eddie's forehead as he tried to keep his leg still. Unable to hold the awkward position any longer, his leg began to wobble. Shaking his head at me, he slowly lifted his foot. I held my breath, waiting for an alarm to go off that would alert everyone to where we were and surely put an end to our sleuthing. Instead, I heard another click and felt the bookcase behind me swing outwards. It was a secret door!

I almost cheered, while Eddie looked like he was going

to throw up. I pushed him into the narrow hallway, closing the bookcase door softly behind me.

'Are you okay?' I whispered.

Gulping in big breaths, he shook his leg. 'Dead leg.'

Taking his hand, I dragged him, hopping on one leg as he shook the other one, around the corner and into a storage area for cabinets and boxes. I pulled us both behind some large paintings leaning against a wall. After catching our breath, I realised I was still holding the book in my hands. So, now I was the thief. Then I remembered what I'd read a few moments earlier.

'Eddie,' I whispered.

'Shhh!'

'No, listen, I found something that will help. Women weren't allowed in the Pavilion until 1999, which I know is totally unfair.' Eddie dutifully nodded his agreement. 'However, there was one exception to the rule and that was for Queen Elizabeth II. And remember Harvey telling us the King and Queen had their own room to sit in?'

'Yeah, it was the Committee Room – so?'

'Well, it says in here that there's supposed to be a secret tunnel for them to use if there's ever an emergency while they're here.'

'Really?' Eddie replied, his eyes growing as big as his grin. 'That must be it.'

8

COVERS

Fielding positions on a batter's offside OR equipment used to protect the pitch from rain

'Come on, let's go,' Eddie said, dragging himself to his feet.

'Okay, just give me a second.' I went back towards the Library and leant the book against a wall, not in plain sight, but somewhere I thought someone might eventually find it. I realised we'd never discovered who was the person that came into the Library. We were on a mission to find the thief and the stolen Urn, but now we had my dad, the police and who knew who else chasing us.

Eddie led me away from the Pavilion towards a door which opened onto a little landing overlooking an empty squash court – yet another sport played here besides cricket! Heading down a staircase, we came to the Real Tennis courts. We continued past them, stopping in front of an emergency exit. Eddie pushed it slightly open then swung it all the way. We were opposite the Coronation Gardens.

'Where are we going?' I asked, totally confused.

'The Committee Room is on the other side of the Pavilion so it's going to be tricky to get there without being seen, especially now the police are here. There's a corridor running along the basement floor of the Pavilion which we can use. We just need to get through the side door.'

'Okay,' I replied, not entirely convinced, but certain that Eddie's mind map was better than mine.

'There was a map of the Pavilion on the wall of the Library and I memorised it.' Eddie grinned at me. Of course he did.

Peeking round the corner, we saw that a policeman was now guarding the Pavilion doors closest to us. As soon as he turned his back to us, Eddie reached out for my hand and started to run, pulling me along. The distance to the Pavilion couldn't have been much longer than a cricket pitch, yet it felt like the never-ending distance to the boundary rope when you were chasing a ball. Looking back up to the Library, I swear I saw a shadow at the window, but couldn't tell who it was. Eddie stopped suddenly, making me crash into him. He held the security card up and the light on the box turned green. Stepping inside, we were at the bottom of a staircase and Eddie put a finger to his lips and pointed up.

'That goes back to Harvey's office,' he whispered.

Heart pounding, I clamped my mouth shut. I couldn't help but feel a little guilty that Dad would be looking frantically for us. All we had to do was go up the little staircase and confess. But we were fully committed now and had to follow through, just like we would if we were running a quick single. Eddie turned left into some empty offices. The view was unbelievable. It looked right across the ground to the Media Centre, and suddenly I knew exactly where we were.

'Eddie, we're under the Bowlers Bar, aren't we? So, this must have been the Professionals' changing room. Cool!'

There were no traces of the old changing room now, just boring computers. Eddie hurried across the room, through a door, and ran down a long corridor. As he reached out to grab the door handle, I grabbed his arm.

'Be careful,' I said. 'You have no idea if anyone is on the other side.'

Thankfully, Eddie hesitated and nodded. He opened it a fraction and peeked through. 'Thank goodness you stopped me. I thought we'd just be able to walk all the way to the other side.'

'Where are we?' I asked him.

'At the bottom of the main staircase, near the doors where the policeman is standing guard. There's toilets and stuff down here and another door opposite us. So, if we can get across to the other door without being seen, we should be okay.'

He watched for a few moments before pushing it open and dashing across the gap. I followed him, keeping one eye on the policeman as I bolted through the opposite door. We dodged boxes and paintings and other discarded random things, and were about halfway down when we heard the door behind us start to open. Eddie jumped through a doorway and quickly out again.

'Argh! It's only a little kitchen with nowhere to hide,' he exclaimed.

'In here,' I said, and disappeared behind a door. It was a room of lost and found, with a row of coats hanging over some old trunks sitting on the floor. I stepped over a trunk and elbowed my way in between two coats. Pulling them back into place, I was completely hidden. Eddie quickly squeezed in next to me. I heard a phone vibrate and a man answer it in a hushed voice. Unaware we were hiding, he paced back and forth in front of our doorway. I risked a little peek through the coat. It was the journalist. I whispered in Eddie's ear who it was.

'I knew it, he's the thief!' Eddie whispered

triumphantly.

I nodded and held my finger in front of my lips to silence him so I could hear what the journalist was saying.

'No, it's all changed. I can't find even a whiff of a scandal with him. But this story is much bigger than that … I don't know for sure, but from what I understand the Urn was stolen and replaced with a replica so no one would discover it …'

I patted Eddie's hand: he'd been right all along. Unfortunately for us, it didn't sound like the journalist was the one who'd stolen it.

'I know, such luck I'm already here, and thanks again for getting me a security card. I'm able to come and go as I please and I'm going to get first dibs on the scoop of the century … No, no suspects yet, the police have just arrived and everyone was herded into the Long Room to be interviewed. I've managed to avoid them so far … The only thing suspicious is the two kids … Yeah, I know, it sounds strange, but the girl is the one who distracted the security guard in the first place when she dropped the replica Urn … I doubt they're involved, but I need to find out what they're up to, just in case. I've followed them to the Library and now they're in the Pavilion.' Eddie and I exchanged a look; at least we now knew who had been in the Library, and now I could add his name to the list of people chasing us. 'Yes, I'll let you know as soon as I have anything new.'

The journalist hung up and continued to stride down the

corridor. As soon as we heard a door close, Eddie turned to me. His face was fuming. 'How could he think we're involved?' he asked. 'He's the one who's been acting suspicious the whole day. Not us.'

I giggled. 'Well, when you think about it, we probably do look suspicious.'

'Huh! I guess so, but still.'

'Well, at least we can strike him off our suspect list. He definitely didn't steal it and is only interested in getting the story.'

'Who does that leave us with, then?' Eddie asked.

I thought about our list and realised we'd only ever had two suspects and they'd both been proven innocent. The only clue we had left was the rat poo, which may or may not have come from the disused train tunnels that may or may not be connected to a secret escape tunnel for the King or Queen. My cheeks flushed as I remembered the book I'd left outside the Library. What if the journalist had found it and made the same connection as us? He wasn't just following us anymore, he knew exactly where we were going, and I'd led him straight to it. I jumped up and pushed through the coats: we couldn't let him find the thief before we did.

'We need to get to the Committee Room and find the secret tunnel before he does,' I said.

'That's if he even knows where we're going.'

For once, I hoped Eddie couldn't read my guilty thoughts. 'Come on, let's go.'

Clicking on the security box at the end of the corridor, we passed through another empty office and into a lobby at the foot of the stairs. An elevator was in one corner, while there were also doors to a kitchen and the men's toilets.

'These stairs should take us to the Committee Room – and remember, it's also next to the Long Room, where the journalist said everyone is, so we need to be careful, okay?' Eddie whispered, pointing up, and I gave him a thumbs-up in acknowledgement.

We climbed one step at a time, peering through the MCC-embossed spindles as we went. Halfway up the first flight, Eddie paused, putting his finger to his lips. A policewoman was standing at the top of the stairs, guarding the Long Room doors. There was no way we could sneak past her and into the Committee Room without being seen. I hunched my shoulders in defeat and saw Eddie's do the same.

Back-tracking down the stairs, the whirr of a hand dryer made us pause, mid-step. Someone was in the men's toilets. Above us, the policewoman heard it too and her feet shuffled forward. Panicking, we backed away from both sounds, not sure where to run. The cool metal of the elevator door pressed against my arm and I swung around, frantically hitting the call button. Finally, the doors slid back and Eddie and I tumbled inside. We heard a shout from the policewoman as her footsteps hurried down the stairs. The last thing we saw before the doors slid shut was the journalist stepping out of the toilet door, his confused face snapping from us to the approaching policewoman and back again.

9

PLAY AND MISS

A batter takes a big swing at the ball, but doesn't hit it

Slumped on the elevator floor, I could hear the journalist through the steel doors and over the sound of my rapidly beating heart. He was shouting, protesting his innocence as to why he wasn't in the Long Room with everyone else. Would he give us up? I really didn't know. Without warning, the elevator doors opened again. Eddie and I launched at the control panel, jabbing the 'close door' button over and over again. We could just see the feet of the journalist and the policewoman as they climbed the stairs. The doors stuttered, then closed once more. Eddie kept his finger firmly on the button.

'Eddie, we need to pick a floor, otherwise the doors will keep opening,' I said, stating the absolute obvious.

'I know, I know, I'm thinking.'

'Well, think faster, as I bet any money that journalist will tell everyone where we are.'

'Well, maybe *you* should think of something for a change.'

'Hey, that's not fair,' I said, wounded by Eddie's sharp words. He'd never, ever spoken to me like that. 'You're the one who made me go on this stupid goose chase.'

'And you're the one who got us into this mess in the first place,' Eddie snapped. His face was flustered, and his shoulders slumped forward as he kept his finger pressed on the elevator button.

I sucked my breath in. I couldn't understand why Eddie was being so cruel. He was the one who'd guessed the Urn was stolen and insisted we follow the flimsiest of clues, not me. I shuffled to the farthest corner of the elevator and turned my back so he couldn't see my tears. I shoved my plait into my mouth and bit down hard. We were supposed to be having the best day of our lives, yet right now I just felt miserable.

After the longest we'd ever gone without speaking, I heard Eddie sigh. 'I'm sorry, Tess, I didn't mean to snap at you. You're right, it's not your fault. I was so sure we could solve the mystery by ourselves. And just now we were so close to getting caught.'

I sniffed, refusing to answer.

'Come on, Tess. It's been so much fun playing detective, hasn't it? I just didn't want it to end. Haven't you been having fun? Don't you want to keep going?'

I shrugged. I guess I had been having lots of fun, and it had been really exciting. We just seemed to be going around in circles. I spat my plait out and slowly turned around to face Eddie. His finger, still pressing the door button, had turned white.

'Fine, but if we're going to keep going, we need to have a plan.'

'Yes!' Eddie made a victory fist. 'And you're right, we need a proper plan.'

I grinned, happy that he and I were friends again. 'And the first thing we need to do is get out of this lift and find somewhere to hide.'

'I agree,' Eddie said, still grinning. 'Let's go back to the lost and found room.'

Safely behind our curtain of coats, Eddie wiggled his finger to get the blood circulating again. 'It's literally impossible to get to the Committee Room and search for the secret tunnel,' he said. 'So, what other clues or information do we have?'

'Well,' I said, checking the points on my fingers. 'We know that the Urn was definitely stolen and replaced with a replica, thanks to the journalist and the fact there's loads of police here.' Eddie nodded. 'Rat poo mysteriously appeared on my shoe after someone pushed past me. We have ruled out our two main suspects and still don't know who it was that stood on my foot or how they got rat poo on their shoe in the first place.'

'So …'

'So, we've discovered there may, or may not, be an emergency secret tunnel, and we think that might be how the thief is getting in and out of Lord's, and that's where they stood in some poo.'

Eddie was silent as he thought over the facts. We'd made so many assumptions, and something about it all was nagging me. And then I realised what it was.

'If there is a tunnel for the King or Queen, what do you think it looks like?' I asked.

'I dunno … A tunnel. Why?'

'Do you really think they would let them escape through any ordinary tunnel, or do you think it would be clean and spiderweb-free and –'

'Rat poo-free! Of course, Tess, you're a genius.' Eddie said. I beamed, pleased at my sleuthing skills. 'The entrance to the train tunnels would be near the train tracks, not under the Pavilion. I'm such a dummy!'

I laughed at Eddie. 'You're not a dummy, we just jumped to all the wrong conclusions without thinking it through. Where do the train tracks run, do you know?'

I watched Eddie's face as he trolled through his memory bank of Tube lines, maps and anything else that would lead us in the right direction. 'Now I remember: they are under the Nursery Ground, which is why the Nursery Pavilion is only a temporary building. The MCC isn't allowed to dig any foundations because they don't own the tunnels underneath.'

Once more I shook my head at Eddie's extraordinary brain and how much information it held.

'What's wrong?'

'Nothing, I was just thinking how cool your brain is.'

Eddie's cheeks blushed under my compliment. 'Thanks … You know it's not always a good thing, right?'

'Yeah, I know, but not today. Today it's our secret weapon against the Urn Thief,' I said with a chuckle, and Eddie broke out into a huge smile.

'Okay,' he said, 'Let's go to the Nursery Ground and see if we can find some kind of entrance. If we don't find anything, then I think we've done all we can and we should go back to your dad.'

My heart hardened with determination. There was no way I was going to let this horrible thief get away with such a terrible crime. I would not let them ruin cricket.

We exited the Pavilion through the same side door we'd come in not all that long ago. Keeping under the shadow of the huge stands as much as we could, we moved stealthily past the mosaic tiles of the Father Time Wall. Straight ahead we could see a man guarding the North Gate, so we continued to our right until we reached the colossal pylons holding up the Media Centre. Hiding behind one, we surveyed the area. Our only route was through the food village between the MCC Academy and the Nursery Ground. It wasn't fair that we had to walk through the food village to get there, either. The most delicious foods smells reminded me we hadn't eaten anything since breakfast.

'I know,' Eddie said, hearing my stomach growl. 'We don't have time to stop and eat, though. Once we've caught the thief we can eat as much as we like.'

'Fine,' I mumbled as my stomach growled again.

Behind the Nursery Pavilion and Academy Centre was a car park and storage area. Our eyes scanned the space, searching for anything that resembled the entrance to the tunnels.

'Over there!' Eddie yelled, then clamped one hand over his mouth and used the other to point towards the corner. Nestled between two industrial bins was a small structure of slanting brick walls with metal doors on top – perfect for hiding a staircase. We hurried over. An open padlock was dangling from the latch. And if we needed any further proof that we were in the right place, I jumped as a rat scuttled out from behind the bins.

'Ready?' Eddie said with the hugest smile on his face.

'Ready,' I replied, my stomach doing somersaults in anticipation.

10

FOLLOW-THROUGH

The motion of the bowler running down the wicket after they bowl the ball

I grabbed my nose as soon as Eddie unlatched the door, as the now familiar smell of rat poo mixed with damp and dirt wafted out. Before us was a metal staircase leading down to what we hoped would be the abandoned train tunnels. The stairs were filthy: totally not fit for the King or Queen to use, emergency or no emergency, so there was absolutely no way they would use this as an escape route. The mythical Secret Tunnel would have to remain a mystery for us to solve another day. On the plus side, the stairs were covered in gooey footprints leading up and down, so it was obvious that someone had used this entrance on more than one occasion, and recently.

'I'll go first,' I said, surprising both myself and Eddie, who gave me a quizzical look. I shrugged. I was never usually so brave. And I couldn't ever remember feeling so excited, but I was growing more and more confident with every clue we found. I really couldn't wait to go down the stairs and find the next one.

'Okay,' Eddie said, 'But keep to the edge of the staircase so you don't ruin the footprints.'

'Oh, good idea.' Tentatively, I stepped onto the first step, trying not to cringe as my foot squished into the muck, not caring that my new trainers were going to be ruined. Well, maybe caring a little, as Mum would kill me. But if it led us to the thief, a spoiled pair of shoes would be worth it. As I descended, I heard millions of scurrying rat feet echoing in the walls. I flinched and paused mid-step, suddenly regretting that I'd wanted to go first.

Eddie grinned. 'I'm sure they're running away, more scared of us than us of them.'

'Huh!' I laughed nervously, continuing down the stairs. Pausing for a second on the bottom step, I stepped onto the scuffed brick floor. Surprisingly, the wall lights were on so I could see I was in the middle of a really large, curve-roofed tunnel. The ceiling and walls were filthy, covered in big black splodges and orange water stains.

Behind me, Eddie descended halfway down the staircase before slamming the doors shut.

'We're not locked in, are we?' I asked, the usual panic starting to bubble in my belly. Eddie pushed on the doors, and I relaxed when a sliver of light appeared. 'Phew, I don't think I could handle being locked down here.'

He closed the doors again and bounded down the remaining steps to stand next to me. He studied the ground. 'There are footprints leading to our right. Come on. Try and stick to the walls so we don't squash them.'

'But there's rats in the walls.'

'The rats are long gone; besides, we don't want to ruin any footprint evidence.'

'Fine,' I said reluctantly, and moved as close to the grimy wall as I dared. However, it wasn't rats that caused me to freeze to the spot. Instead, the ground trembled beneath my feet, and I looked to Eddie, dreading that he was going to confirm what I'd already suspected.

'There's no tracks in here,' Eddie said, easing my worries only slightly. 'The trains must be on the other side of the walls, or below us or something. We should be okay.'

'Should be?' I snapped, a little too sharply, as I waited for my heartbeat to return to normal. Between rats and trains I was beginning to think this was a really stupid idea. I soon forgot about following footprints, and the horrible rat smells, and wondered how long this tunnel could go on for. I only jumped when I felt the rumble of a train and a gentle breeze tickling my hair. Without warning, a brick wall appeared, blocking our way.

'I can't believe it,' Eddie exclaimed. 'There has to be another way out; we must have missed a door or something.'

'Yep, there's only our footprints here,' I agreed, examining the ground. 'We need to go back.'

We did a U-turn and, keeping our eyes glued to the ground, retraced our footprints. The trains kept rumbling past and when I felt the breeze on my face again, I realised this was the exact same spot I'd felt the breeze before. My eyes darted across the floor until I found what I was looking for. A huge grin spread on my face.

'Look,' I simply said, pointing to the trail of footprints that could be seen as clearly as the first footprints on the moon. There were three distinct sets: tiny ones from my new shoes, huge ones from Eddie's, and some that were in between which must have belonged to the thief. While mine and Eddie's kept walking straight ahead, the other set turned at a right angle and went towards the wall, or, to be more precise, two white doors. How had we missed them?

Eddie shouted a massive 'Woohoo' that echoed along the walls then bounced back to us. I shushed him and we both giggled.

11

FOOTWORK

When a batter moves their feet to be in the correct position to hit the ball

I had to stand on tiptoes to peer through the two little windows in the doors. I could see a set of train tracks and beyond them an empty platform. If this was a Tube station, where were all the people? I'd never, ever been on a Tube platform when there had been no other people. The ground began to rattle as a breeze wafted through the little gap in the door. The screech of wheels got louder until it was almost unbearable. I covered my ears as the train rushed past, inches away from our faces. The backdraft sucked the flimsy doors inwards, making them flap. Reaching out, I clutched Eddie's arm to anchor me in case I got sucked through the gap.

'Come on, we need to get across to the platform before the next train comes.'

'Are you crazy?' I shouted, dropping my hand from his arm. 'Did you not see that train and how close it was?'

'Yeah, of course. We'll have to time it, but we should be able to get across. How often do you think the trains go? Every two or three minutes?'

I stared at Eddie, for once unable to speak to him. We couldn't just walk across the train tracks. What on earth was he thinking?

'It'll be fine, Tess. I'm just counting now to see how long before the next train, and then we can make a plan.'

'Eddie!' I screeched. 'This is ridiculous. We'll get electrocuted.'

'Not if we don't touch the tracks,' Eddie replied matter-of-factly. 'It's only a few feet across. We'll have plenty of time.'

I was fuming. Eddie wasn't thinking straight.

'And what happens if you do touch the tracks? What am I supposed to do then? What am I supposed to say to your dad or your mum? "Oh yeah, we knew the Urn had been stolen so we snuck around Lord's, then went down into the rat-infested tunnels and decided we could cross the Tube tracks. Sorry, we didn't mean for Eddie to get electrocuted."'

Eddie rolled his eyes. 'Come on, Tess, stop being so dramatic. I'm not going to get electrocuted, and neither are you. It'll be just like taking a quick single. Put your head down, watch where you step, and you'll be on the other side before you know it.'

I exhaled through my nose like an angry fast bowler who'd just been hit for six. 'And what do you reckon we're going to find on the other side of the platform anyway? The thief will be long gone by now.'

That made Eddie pause for a couple of seconds, making me think I was getting through to him. Not!

'Maybe, but we've come this far and I don't want to go back. We owe it to ourselves to keep going.'

I was about to retort when the ground rumbled again and Eddie held his hand up to silence me, just as I'd seen his mum do to him a million times. This time, neither of us flinched when the train roared past.

'Three minutes, that's plenty of time,' Eddie stated. I turned and started walking away. Excited as I was that we'd followed the clues to get here, there was absolutely no way I was going to cross those tracks.

'Tess, wait.' Eddie grabbed my arm. 'Come on, we're supposed to be Cricket Detectives and good detectives always take risks.'

'Taking risks means nearly getting caught by the police in the Pavilion, not going on a suicide mission.'

Eddie's face dropped. 'It's not a suicide mission. We have plenty of time if we time it right. The thief is on the other side, I just know it. We're so close and can't give up now. We're the only ones who can find the Urn and save cricket.'

I poked my finger through one of my plaits. Dang it! He was right. We really were so close, and I really wanted to find the Urn and see who the Urn Thief was. Urgh! Being a Cricket Detective was harder than I thought. 'Fine!' I moaned.

Eddie's face lit up. 'Really?'

I poked my tongue out and gruffly opened the doors a fraction. I could see we would have to cross three tracks to get to the other side, and then climb up the platform. I guess it didn't look too hard … And I trusted Eddie. 'How long 'til the next train?'

The ground rumbled in answer, and I closed the door, bracing myself. Eddie and I locked eyes and nodded. As soon as it passed, we thrust the doors open and Eddie shouted, 'Run!'

I watched as Eddie's long legs leapfrogged the rails with ease. My shorter legs refused to go as fast, and I cautiously lifted one as high as possible and straddled the first track. I felt better when I saw there was a big gap between my legs and the track. More confidently, I swung my other leg over – I had cleared the first one. I was confident I could cross the other two the same way, until I saw the small hole. It was a pit of some kind under the middle rail. I knew my legs weren't going to be long enough to step over it. Thinking quick, I dropped to my knees and crawled under the rail. I shuddered as the metal fizzed with electricity barely inches from my head.

'Come on, slowpoke,' Eddie grinned as he grabbed hold of the platform ready to climb out. I scowled back at him. His face change to shock as he jerked his left leg up and down. It was stuck on something.

'Tess, help!'

I froze. How was I supposed to help him? He was the one who was always helping me. Eddie's face pleaded with me. I had to do something; I couldn't let him down now. Not after everything he'd done for me and not when he needed me most. He was my best friend. I had to save him. Springing into action, I leapt out from the pit to Eddie's side.

'Help me, Tess. Help, I'm stuck.' Eddie was getting hysterical, but I felt surprisingly calm.

Placing one foot either side of the track, I squatted (making a mental note to smugly tell Mum that a dress would have been ridiculously inappropriate for this particular situation), and studied Eddie's foot carefully. It was hard to see in the dark tunnel, but it looked like his shoelace had wrapped itself around one of the big bolts.

'Stay still,' I shouted, and Eddie immediately froze. I couldn't tell if it was because he was so scared or because he'd never heard me shout before. All I needed to do was reach down and wriggle the shoelace off the bolt and everything would be fine. I squatted as low as I could over the metal rail. Curling my fingers under the bolt, I began to wriggle the shoelace loose. It was stuck pretty tight, but after a couple of wiggles I finally felt it starting to give. I looked up to Eddie and nodded; he gave me a weak smile of encouragement, although his eyes remained panicked. It was hard work, and soon my finger began to cramp and my thighs began to ache. The lace was almost at the end of the bolt. My thighs burned even more and sweat started to squeeze out of every pore in my body. The breeze on my face was a welcome relief, and I lifted my head towards it to cool me down.

As I did, I felt the ground beneath my feet begin to shake. The tunnel that was so black before now had the smallest light, growing brighter and brighter. My heart skipped a beat then pounded a million times faster. I glanced at Eddie again and could literally see the colour drain from his face. He checked his watch.

'Thirty seconds.'

Oh no!

Eddie yanked his foot, undoing all the good work I'd done. 'Eddie, you've got to stay still.' My voice cracked as I shouted at him. Seizing his ankle tight, I held it in place as I wriggled the shoelace faster and faster.

'I can't, Tess, the train's coming. I'm so sorry, I should have listened to you. We're going to die and it's all my fault.' Eddie was sobbing.

I inhaled and blocked out all the noise around me – just

as Dad had taught me to do when batting. He always said if I could block everything out and focus on the bowler running in and nothing else, then I had more of a chance of getting bat on ball. Focusing on the lace, I wriggled and wriggled it until it got to the end of the bolt. But even if I did slip it off, would there be time to climb up to the platform?

'Twenty seconds, Tess. Hurry!'

Out of the corner of my eye I spied the pit under the middle track. If only …

Eddie started screaming. The noise of the train grew louder. The bolt vibrated violently under my fingers. If I didn't pull the lace off now it would slip back on, even tighter. The train's headlight lit up the tunnel, making the white shoelace stand out against the dark bolt. With one last yank, the lace slipped off. I dragged Eddie down, slipped into the pit and closed my eyes.

12

NOT OUT

The umpire says this when they are turning down an appeal for a wicket

The train rushed over us, barely inches from our faces. The noise was unbearable, and I shuddered along with the motion of the train. It had been really stupid trying to cross the tracks. What had we been thinking? Sure, I'd saved Eddie's life, but we weren't out of danger yet: the next train would be here soon. Would we have time to crawl out and get to the platform before it came? We had to. Next to me, Eddie was shaking and weeping quietly. I reached for his hand and gave it little a squeeze before tugging on it to get up.

'Come on, Eddie, we need to move.' He didn't budge. 'Eddie, come on. We haven't got long until the next train.'

'I can't.'

'Yeah, you can. We just have to time it and watch that our shoelaces don't get stuck!' I laughed at my own joke, which Eddie didn't find as funny. I gave his hand another squeeze. I could hear a train in the distance and felt the ground rumble. Eddie stiffened again, knowing we wouldn't have time to move. 'It'll be fine. We're already halfway across so we'll have heaps of time after the next train. Just close your eyes and stay still.'

I braced myself as the train thundered over us.

This time I didn't give Eddie a choice as I pulled him out of our hidey-hole. He wiped his eyes and sniffed before reluctantly following me out of the pit. Very carefully, we stepped over the last track, and I hauled myself up onto the platform. I reached out for Eddie's hand and helped him up before dragging him across the platform. Eddie slumped against the wall, and I collapsed next to him.

'You okay?' I asked.

He shrugged. 'Yeah, I guess.'

'Cool.'

'Tess, you saved my life,' he whispered.

I bumped his shoulder. 'No worries.'

He was still sniffing a little so I decided to distract him by asking what we should do next. 'Dunno,' was his sullen reply.

Even though he was shaken, I still thought Eddie would know what to do next. But what if he didn't snap out of it? I had no idea what we should do. Then again, I'd just saved his life so maybe I was more capable of doing things than I thought. I was actually really proud of myself. Eddie had needed me, and I hadn't hesitated. I looked over at him. He was still pale and trying to hold back tears. It really was up to me to decide what we did next. I gulped down a wave of panic. I'd never had to lead anyone before. It didn't matter; I had to do this for Eddie.

I studied the train station, trying to come up with a plan. Filthy stalactites hung from the concrete roof, while the walls were smeared with dirt and dust. My heart leapt as I saw a trail of footprints, the same as we'd seen in the tunnels, running down the middle of the platform to a metal fence and a staircase. Someone had been here! Thank goodness, as I was starting to think this had all been for nothing.

I nudged Eddie playfully in the side. Normally, he would groan and pretend that tiny little me had hurt him. But he didn't flinch. I sucked in a deep breath.

'Eddie, there's more footprints this way. Let's go.' Eddie still didn't move. 'Come on, we're getting closer.'

Nothing.

'Eddie, I know you've had a really big scare, but you're

okay. I'm okay too. You've got to suck it up. I can't do it on my own.'

'No!'

'No? No, what?'

'No, I'm not okay and no, I'm not going any farther.'

'But …'

'But nothing, Tess. I nearly died. This whole thing is stupid and a big mistake.'

I flicked my plait back and forth before shoving it in my mouth. I had to get through to him, but how? I chewed and chewed until inspiration hit and I knew what I had to say.

'Do you remember the first day we met?' I asked.

Eddie shrugged.

'Davey and James were being really mean to me, teasing me about my accent and yelling, "Keep on walking, Walker". But you stood up to them even though they were older than us.'

'So?'

'And remember when Sally locked me out of the changing rooms because she said I was too little to play? You stormed right up, banged on the door, and told her I'd scored more runs than she had, and she needed to grow up. She never did anything to me again after that. Well, the point is, you've always had my back and today I had yours. So, let's just say we're even and get on with finding the Urn. Besides, we can't go back as I really don't think you want to cross the tracks again, so we have to keep going forward.'

Eddie stared across the tracks and shuddered. 'We're not even close to being even, Tess,' he whispered. 'You literally saved my life. All I've ever done was tell a few bullies to cut it out. It's totally not the same.'

'Well, Edward Armstrong. I totally think it is the same. And besides, the only thing that matters is that we keep having each other's back. That's what best friends are for. Now, stop snivelling and let's follow these footprints.'

Eddie sniffed and wiped his eyes. 'Alright, then, Teresa Walker. I didn't know you could be such a pain in the bum. And so bossy, for that matter.'

I grinned back with a huge sigh of relief. Everything was going to be okay. Reluctantly, Eddie stood up and followed me down the platform. As we neared the end, a breeze blew up and a rumble came down the track. Eddie's face dropped, so I quickened our pace, ready to climb the white, brick-lined staircase, which led to a metal door. The footprints didn't go up the stairs; instead, they stopped in front of a door labelled 'Relay Room'. A light was shining out from under the door, and I could hear shuffling inside. This was our moment of truth. Either we'd stumbled upon an Underground worker, or we were about to come face to face with our Urn Thief.

13

YORKER

A very fast ball that is bowled on the batter's toes

I looked to Eddie to see if he was going to go first. He didn't move. It was up to me; I crept closer to the door. I bent down to peer through the small keyhole. The room was a grey colour, lined on one side with ceiling-to-floor cupboards full of a jumble of old cords and cables. Against the other wall was a long bench. Someone was standing in front of it, stuffing papers into a bag. I caught my breath and drew away, bumping into Eddie who was hovering behind.

'What?!?' Eddie whispered. 'What did you see?'

I couldn't speak as I processed exactly what I had seen. Ever since Eddie had convinced me that the Urn had actually been stolen, I'd pictured the thief to be some dastardly, horrible-looking man with a jagged scar on his face. Instead, the person I saw was a lady with red hair wearing black clothing. Shock jolted through me. It couldn't be, could it? Suddenly, it all made sense.

Eddie was staring at me with his palms spread out, waiting for an answer. I didn't have one yet, I needed to have another look first. Slowly, I bent down and put my eye back to the keyhole. The lady had moved, letting me see the bench more clearly. It was covered in scattered newspaper clippings and pages ripped from books. Stuck to the wall above it were photos of the Urn, a big house, and two people in old-fashioned clothes. There were also maps of Lord's and the Underground. A notebook lay on the bench and, if I needed any further proof that we'd tracked down the Urn thief, the Urn was sitting perilously close to the edge of the bench. Thankfully, it was still in one piece. Anger raged through me. How dare this horrible lady think she could steal the Urn and get away with it?

'What can you see?' Eddie asked again.

'Shh! I can see the Urn.'

'Are you sure it's the real one and not another fake?'

I nodded. 'I've seen enough fake ones today to know

this is real.'

An eye appeared on the other side of the keyhole, making me jump back. The door flew open. Before I could react, the lady seized my arm and dragged me into the tiny room. She turned and grabbed Eddie and threw him next to me. Eddie's eyes grew larger than a cricket ball as he took in everything I'd seen through the keyhole.

Our thief, the person who'd pushed past me as they tried to escape, stepping on my shoe and leaving a smelly clue in the process, was none other than the security guard who was carrying the Urn from the Museum to the Long Room. Of course! Why hadn't we put her on our suspect list? She had the perfect opportunity to switch the Urn when she removed it from the glass box. It was the perfect crime. And no one would have noticed if I hadn't distracted her, making her drop it. So, now we knew the means, we just needed to find out the motive.

'Who are you? What are you doing here?' the lady asked in a controlled voice that sent a shiver down my spine. I couldn't believe that I'd felt sorry for her only hours earlier when the journalist had been yelling at her. She was the evil one, not him. This time I wouldn't stay silent. Brimming with new-found confidence, I opened my mouth to speak. However, my voice caught in my throat and a gurgle was the only thing that came out. The lady grinned mockingly at me, causing me to take a step back and hang my head in shame.

Sensing my distress, Eddie finally snapped out of his

trance and moved protectively in front of me. 'You stole the Urn,' he stated.

The lady's eyes turned from shock to panic as they darted to the Urn then back to Eddie. She faltered for a moment and then her eyes blazed with anger.

'It belongs to me,' she replied, her voice only slightly quavering as she thrust her bottom lip out in defiance.

'Ha! You're joking, right?' Eddie mocked. My fists curled into tight balls at my sides even though I was still unable to speak. I couldn't believe I was back to being so timid after literally just saving Eddie's life.

'I am not joking, you impertinent little brat,' the lady replied. 'I have proof – there.' She pointed to the diary on the bench.

I knew that whatever proof she was talking about had to be false. Alan had literally told us the REAL story behind the Urn this morning. Whatever she was saying now had to be lies.

'Look, you obviously think the Urn belongs to you, but it doesn't. It belongs to Lord's and everyone who loves cricket,' Eddie said.

'No. It. Doesn't. It belongs to me.'

Eddie took one step closer to her, but I touched his arm. We knew this woman was a thief, but we didn't know if she was dangerous. He understood, and stopped.

'Okay, so let's all calm down. I'm Eddie, this is Tess, and, according to your name tag, you're Hazel Croft. There's obviously been a misunderstanding. You work at

Lord's as a security guard so is that why you think the Urn belongs to you?'

'No, I took a job with the security company so I could take back what belongs to me.'

Both Eddie and I gasped at her confession. I couldn't believe we'd actually done it. We'd literally found the Urn Thief and she'd made a full confession. We'd been better detectives than even Sherlock Holmes. But what were our next steps? We hadn't planned this far ahead, and I didn't have my phone to call Dad or the police and they had no idea where we were. Perhaps we could distract her, grab the Urn and make a run for the top of the stairs? I looked at Eddie and he shook his head. Okay, bad plan. Maybe we could talk her round instead? Only, I couldn't just leave all the talking to Eddie. For once in my life I needed to speak up.

'Proof.' It was barely above a whisper and sounded croaky, but at least I'd gotten something out.

'What did you say?' Hazel rudely retorted, and I felt myself blush.

'Proof,' Eddie chipped in, and relief rushed through me. 'We need proof why you think the Urn is yours.'

Hazel eyed us both before giving us a little nod. Picking up the diary, she shoved it in our faces.

'This is my great-great-grandmother's diary. She was a maid at Cobham Hall when Ivo Bligh was the earl. She wrote in here that the earl was going to leave the Urn to her when he died. Instead, it was given to the MCC. My family was robbed and now I want it back.'

I shook my head at this information. I didn't know too much about relationships between earls and maids, but I would bet any money that they didn't normally leave things to them in their wills – especially something that your wife had given to you. Not only did the Urn symbolise Ivo and Florence's love, it also symbolised the unique bond between English and Australian cricket. Something wasn't adding up.

Eddie seemed to agree with me. He snatched the diary and started flicking through the pages. I peered over his shoulder. The diary was in really good condition considering it was supposed to be over 100 years old. The paper still looked new, not faded and yellowy like I'd seen in old books in museums. 'Are you sure that's her diary? I mean, I didn't think many maids back then could read, let alone write,' Eddie said.

He realised his mistake as soon as Hazel's eyes darkened and narrowed. She leaned in close to him and snatched the diary back. 'Are you saying my great-great-granny was stupid?'

'No, no, not at all,' Eddie cried, desperately trying to back-track. 'Of course she could read and write. What would I know? I'm just a dumb kid.'

'W-w-w-what Eddie means,' I stuttered, still not quite finding my voice. 'Is-is-is-is that we thought Florence gave the Urn to Ivo because sh-sh-sh-she loved him?'

'Now you think I'm a liar?' I shook my head vigorously

and blushed once more. 'Here, take a look if you don't believe me.'

Hazel flicked through the pages until she found the one she wanted, and then handed it to me. The writing was small and spidery, and very hard to read.

... I was dusting in the Library today and knocked the old vase right off the mantelpiece into the grate. The cork popped out and some ashes spilled all over the hearth. I quickly scooped up some more from the fireplace and refilled it before putting it back in its place. I didn't know My Lord was there and saw the whole thing. He laughed saying how stricken I looked. 'It doesn't matter, Young Mary,' he said to me. 'It's a stupid old thing anyway and now it's chipped, too. You can have it when I die.' I was shocked but secretly happy as I've always loved that vase.

I dropped my hands, puzzled and confused. It sounded like he didn't care at all about the Urn. It couldn't be true. Except it was written right here in front of me.

'See, I told you it belongs to my family,' Hazel said, her eyes still blazing in defiance.

'I don't know,' Eddie replied, scratching the top of his head. 'It still doesn't seem legit.'

I began to flick through the diary. All the other entries were about the jobs she did, like emptying the chamber pots (urgh!) and changing the beds, and silly household gossip. There didn't seem to be any other references to the

Urn, nor the fact that Mary had always loved it.

'W-w-where did you get this from?' I held the diary up to her. I was starting to think it was as fake as the urn I'd made her drop.

'None of your business,' Hazel snapped, crossing her arms in front of her chest.

Eddie peered over my shoulder. 'It doesn't look very old,' he said. I smiled, knowing Eddie understood what I was getting at.

Hazel remained composed but refused to meet our eye. 'Like I said, it's none of your business.'

It was obvious she was hiding something, but I couldn't work out what it was. I cleared my throat and tried to reason with her again. 'We don't mean to be rude. We're j-j-j-just trying to understand what's going on, that's all.'

Finally, she sighed and answered. 'I don't know where it came from. It arrived in the post one day with a note and phone number.'

Eddie and I exchanged a puzzled look then turned back to Hazel.

'What did the note say?' Eddie asked incredulously.

Hazel squirmed before answering. 'It was from a man who said that he'd come across the diary while doing research and had tracked me down as Mary's only living relative. He thought I should rightfully have the Urn and he knew how to help me get it. So, I called him.'

I exchanged another look with Eddie. This woman was seriously gullible. Hadn't she ever heard of Stranger

Danger?

'And you believed him?' Eddie said, spreading his palms out in disbelief.

'Course I did. I knew full well my great-great-granny was a maid at Cobham Hall. Why wouldn't I believe him?'

'For starters, why would he have the diary in the first place and not you? And secondly, why would he even care whether the Urn belonged to you or not?' Eddie replied, ticking them off on his fingers.

'Y-y-y-y-you're not telling us the whole truth, are y-y-you?' I asked.

She shuffled her feet around, looking more uncomfortable than a Number 11 coming in to face the opening bowler swinging the new ball both ways. She snatched the diary out of my hands. 'Well, he might have mentioned there was something inside the Urn that he wanted and was willing to share it with me if I got the Urn for him and then he'd let me keep the Urn.'

'Something inside the Urn? Other than ashes?' I tried to shout, but my voice was still refusing to cooperate, and it continued to come out croaky. 'You're great-great-granny literally says here that it's ashes from a fireplace. Nothing else.'

And then it hit me. If this was true, then the bails that Florence burnt and gave to Ivo weren't in there. Did that make the whole Ashes story a lie? What were the players really playing for? Alan had said they had never even looked inside, so how could anyone know for sure? And did it even matter? It was more about the love story behind the Urn and what it represented than what was actually inside. Wasn't it? Either way, my heart broke a little.

'I don't know exactly,' Hazel replied. 'He didn't tell me. But he gave me all this information about the Urn, got me the job with the security company knowing they worked at Lord's. Even gave me the replica and told me how and when to swap them and how to escape if things didn't go to plan. So, it must be something really special to go to all that trouble. He made me practice for months so I'd get it right. I wasn't expecting …'

Hazel stopped speaking and stared straight at me. Her face contorted into a painful expression before her eyes flashed with anger.

'You! Now I remember. You were the brat who made me drop the replica Urn. You flashed your camera right in my eyes and made me trip up. I'd already done all the hard work switching them and all I had to do was place the fake one in the Long Room and walk away. No one would have noticed until it was too late, and I would have been long gone. But you ruined everything. How did you even find me?'

'Rat poo.' Eddie answered with a shrug.

'Rat poo?' Hazel shrieked, and in one movement scooped her bag off the table and launched it at Eddie's feet. It was the perfect yorker, and Eddie went down, taking me with him. I watched as Hazel grabbed the Urn, smashed the lightbulb and fled through the door, locking it behind her.

The room went pitch black.

14

BAD LIGHT

The umpires take the players off the field when the light has faded and the ball becomes too hard to see

I counted to ten, willing the lights to come back on. Nothing. I closed my eyes and opened them again. It was no use: the lights were still out. I couldn't see or hear anything other than the abnormally loud beating of my heart.

'I'm really scared, Eddie,' I whispered.

Eddie began to untangle himself from me so that we

eventually sat side by side. He fumbled for my hand and squeezed it once he found it. 'Me too.'

My eyes had begun to adjust slightly so I could see the outline of the grey cupboards. At least that gave me some kind of bearing of the room. Not that it helped; no one else knew we were here. And there was still only one door out and that was still locked. Eddie jumped to his feet and felt his way to the door. Twisting and turning the handle, he pulled and pushed it. It didn't budge. He slapped his hands against it before coming to sit back next to me.

'We've got to find a way out of here,' I said hopelessly.

'I know. On the bright side, can you believe we actually found the thief,' Eddie said. 'I mean, I had my suspicions that it must be a fake when it didn't break, but I literally didn't believe we'd find who took it. It was all a bit of fun to see how far we could go.'

'Huh! Me too, but if we can work it out, that means Dad, or the police, will be able to too. We'll just have to wait for them to come. I'm sure it won't be that long.'

I hope I sounded more convinced than I actually was. The truth was that it was the rat poo on my shoe that had led us here and Dad didn't know about that so how was he going to find us, really? How could he possibly know where we were? We'd had our chance to tell him when he'd seen us in the Library. We thought we were being so clever playing detectives like it was some silly game. But now we could literally never be found and die in here. I gulped back tears.

'Yeah, you're right. We just need to sit tight and wait,' Eddie replied.

The ground began to rumble. Eddie clutched my hand, clenching it super-tight. Just when I thought he was going to crush it, the train was gone and he let go. I gave it a little wriggle to make sure I was okay.

Still shaking my hand, I turned my thoughts back to Hazel. Even though we'd solved the case, Hazel and whoever she was working with had gotten away with it. They would both be long gone by the time we were found, if ever. Whoever the other person was, we literally had no idea. He must be very powerful to persuade Hazel to do all the dirty work for him. How could she be so stupid? I was so angry at her. Who in their right mind would believe some random person who called them out of the blue with such a bonkers story? And what did they think was inside the Urn? I thought the Urn was priceless as it was, so it must be something really important if this person had gone to so much trouble to get it. At least we knew who Hazel was, so the police would be able to track her down and make her tell them who she was working with. If we ever got out of here to tell them.

The banging of an outside door snapped me out of my thoughts. I moved closer to Eddie as muffled voices, shouting at each other, filtered through the locked door.

'What's going on?' I whispered.

'I don't know – hopefully it's a worker who's found Hazel and they're telling her off for being here,' Eddie replied.

'That means they'll find us too,' I said, my spirits soaring. I opened my mouth to call out, but before I could shout someone screamed loud enough to be heard through the door. I hastily closed it shut again. I flinched as we heard a thump and the clatter of metal. Pressing myself against Eddie, my heart beat faster than it ever had before. Whatever was going on sounded much more serious than a worker stumbling upon Hazel.

'Eddie –'

'Shh!'

I shoved my plait into my mouth and clamped it shut so tight my jaw started to hurt. Clinging to each other, we waited and waited for someone to come through our door, not sure whether that would be a good or bad thing. As much as I wanted to be rescued, whoever was on the other side sounded really dangerous. No one came, and we heard no other noises. Eventually, I loosened my grip on Eddie's arm and relaxed my aching jaw. I'd been biting so hard on my plait that I wouldn't have been surprised if I'd bitten right through it. Luckily it came out of my mouth in one piece.

'I think they've gone,' Eddie said after a few minutes of silence.

'What do you think happened out there?'

'I don't know. But someone will find us.'

'Are you sure?'

'Hundred per cent.'

I hoped Eddie was right and we hadn't missed our chance of being saved. All we could do was wait.

Trains continued to rumble by like clockwork and I started to count between each one to fill in the time. It took five trains before I heard the scratching. 'Eddie, please tell me that noise is you moving your feet?'

I sweated on his answer as my heart rate skyrocketed once more. Before he could, the scratching noise became louder and seemed to be coming from lots of different directions. Something brushed past my leg.

'Rats! Rats! Rats!' I shouted hysterically, jumping up. My arms flailed as I tried to feel my way to the bench. If I could reach it and climb onto it, I would be safe. My fingers touched something soft and sticky – a spider's web? I screamed again and flapped my arms and legs about. I heard Eddie cry out in pain as I accidentally kicked him.

'Urgh! Ouch! Tess, calm down!' he shouted at me, but I couldn't hear him as my brain was screaming inside my head. Eddie's hand grabbed me and I shrieked and struck it away, hitting him in the nose.

'Ouch, Tess, you've got to stop!'

This time his voice registered, and I stopped dead in my tracks, every muscle rigid. My head throbbed from spinning and my fingers hurt where I'd punched Eddie in the nose. I winced; it must have hurt him too.

'Okay, Tess, that's it. Stay calm.' Eddie's soothing voice started to work its magic even though my heart still pounded. I shivered, certain I could feel spiders crawling over me and rats nibbling at my feet. 'I'm going to reach out for your hand, okay? So don't freak out.'

I nodded, then realised he couldn't see me. 'Okay.'

Eddie's hand brushed mine and I tried not to snatch it away. Instead, I sucked in a deep breath and gripped it tight.

'Great, now I'm right against the bench, so come to me and we'll jump up onto it together and then we'll be safe.'

''Cause rats can't climb, can they?'

'Nope.'

I nodded again then smiled weakly. Tentatively, I slid my foot across the floor as Eddie pulled me along, inch by inch, to the bench. When my hand touched the solid wooden top, the air that I'd been holding came gushing out of me with relief. I scrambled up then tucked my knees under my chin. Eddie jumped up next to me. We'd made it. But what now? We were still locked in a dark room in an abandoned train station with rats scurrying in the walls around us. I began counting between trains again, to distract myself from my illogical thoughts. Finally, I felt calm enough to speak.

'Thanks, Eddie, I really freaked out, didn't I.'

'Yeah … Don't worry about it. I don't like rats that much either. Besides, we're a team, remember; I save you and you save me.'

I smiled and the scared knot in my belly loosened a little. 'We'll be safe up here until someone finds us?' I asked.

'Yep, I'm sure it won't take long. Do you want to play Cricket Team while we wait?' Eddie asked.

'I don't have my phone, remember,' I replied with a sigh.

'Oh yeah, sorry.'

I shifted my bottom back against the wall, wondering just how long it would be before someone figured out where we were. If only we had a torch or something. Then I had a light-bulb moment.

'Wait! What? Oh, my goodness, you've got your phone!'

'Yeah, but you haven't got yours so we can't play?'

'Eddie!' I said, my frustration boiling over. 'Your phone has a torch on it!'

'Oh yeah, sorry,' Eddie replied meekly. He fiddled next to me, and without warning a bright light flooded the room, blinding me. I didn't care – I'd never, ever been so happy to see a light. Then I had another, more important, thought.

'Eddie! You've had your phone the whole time? We can call for help!' I punched him in the arm. How could we have been so stupid? 'Have you got any service?'

Eddie groaned and held the torch away from his face so I couldn't see him blush. 'Sorry, Tess, I forgot I had it.'

'Oh well,' I replied with a grin. 'Let's get out of here.'

Holding it high above him, he moved it back and forth before sighing. 'Nope, there mustn't be any service in the tunnels, and my battery's nearly dead too.'

Great, just great!

Eddie flashed the torch around while I scanned the room searching for another escape route. I cringed when I saw a pair of red eyes peeping out at me and hugged my legs even tighter. Anything to avoid looking at the rats, I picked up a bundle of papers from the desk. Hazel had accumulated so much information on the Urn, including photographs and newspaper articles. They all said the Urn had a mysterious owner. Were they true? Or had someone fabricated them like the diary? It didn't matter, Hazel had been gullible enough to believe them. Maybe that was why the man had chosen her.

Rifling through the remaining items on the desk, my fingers grazed something squishy. A mouldy sandwich. Urgh! I slapped it away and watched it land in a far corner. After a couple of seconds, one rat appeared and nibbled the sandwich. Then a second. And a third. Without warning, high-pitched screeching echoed around the room as hundreds of rats swarmed on the sandwich, fighting each other for every last crumb. The smell was worse than the poo that had been on my shoe, even worse than the rotting sandwich.

I grabbed the neck of my shirt and shoved it over my mouth, then covered my ears with my hands. Shrinking as far away from them as possible, I couldn't drag my eyes away as we watched in horror, scared to move more than an inch in case they turned on us. After only seconds, the rats dispersed as quickly as they came. All that remained was the plastic wrapper. What if no one found us? We'd start to go mouldy just like that sandwich and the rats would eat us alive.

'Eddie, we have to get out of here. Now!' My voice remained steady as I fought off the rising hysteria.

Eddie nodded. 'The rats must be getting in from somewhere. Maybe that can be our way out too?'

I shook my head. 'There is absolutely no way I'm going anywhere near those rats. We have to find another way.'

Swinging my head back and forth, I looked around. There was no other obvious exit. Feeling slightly manic, I jumped off the bench and shoulder-charged the door. It didn't budge and I felt pain radiate down my arm. I bashed it again and again, not caring that it hurt. Eddie joined me and we thumped and thumped until our shoulders went numb. Still the door hadn't moved. I sank to the floor, rubbing my arm. It was useless, we weren't strong enough. I was breathing fast and I felt another wave of panic sweep through my body. Could we be running out of air? Maybe we'd suffocate? Surely that had to be better than being eaten alive by rats?

Eddie nudged me and pointed to the bench. 'Do you think we could break off one of the legs and use it to smash the lock or something?'

'Sure, we've got nothing to lose.'

Taking turns, we kicked and kicked the leg until the screws came loose and the top and everything on it came crashing to the floor. Eddie picked up the leg and wedged the flattest end between the lock and the door. Gripping hard, he nodded to me.

'Ready?' he said, and I nodded determinedly. 'Pull!'

We heaved the leg back and forth so many times I lost count. My arm that was numb only moments ago now had pins and needles running up and down it. Sweat beaded on my forehead and my breathing grew more and more difficult. I didn't think I could go on much longer when I heard the first crack and saw the wood splinter. Yes! With renewed vigour, I poured every last ounce of energy into the metal leg.

I could hear more cracks as the wood began to give way. With one last heave, the wood split, breaking the lock, and the door swung free. We crashed through it, gasping for breath.

15

BREAKTHROUGH

The bowling team takes a wicket after two batters have batted together for a long time and made lots of runs

I doubled over, resting my hands on my knees, gulping in air before dropping my arms down, shaking them to get the blood pumping again. Even though I ached all over, I was ecstatic to be out of that ghastly little room. Eddie was also doubled over, sucking in big breaths. I straightened and took a step towards him. Something cracked, and I froze. Glancing down, I could see Eddie's phone squashed underneath my foot. I bent down to pick it up, hoping that it wasn't broken; Eddie's phone was our last chance of help. My whole body slumped when I saw how badly the screen was cracked. This was really bad. Eddie looked from the broken phone to my face, and burst out laughing.

'Oh, Tess, you should see the look on your face.'

I scowled. This was no laughing matter.

'It's not my phone, silly.' He laughed again, going back into the little room to retrieve his phone.

How stupid! Of course it wasn't his phone. I clearly remember him propping up the light so we'd have free hands to break through the door. I bent to pick up the broken phone. If it wasn't Eddie's, then whose was it? In reply, I heard a long, painful groan. Every single hair on my body stood on end. I glanced at Eddie in time to see the colour rush from his face, knowing his terrified expression mirrored my own. Neither of us moved, neither of us breathed.

'It's just a train,' I whispered, not sure if I was trying to convince him or myself. Eddie looked puzzled then nodded, despite his face being totally unconvinced. Yes, that's all it was, I told myself: nothing but the screech of wheels on a track. Then I heard it again. Not a train, and most definitely human.

'Help. Help me.'

Very slowly, I turned my head towards the sound. The first thing I saw was a fire extinguisher lying at the bottom of the stairs. Even more slowly, I moved my eyes up the stairs, one step at a time, until they reached the top. I shrieked as I saw Hazel's face covered in blood, her eyes staring blankly at me. Then she blinked and reached a bloody hand out towards me.

'Help me.'

I was too terrified to move. Who had attacked her, and why? That must have been the fight we'd heard. And what if that person was still here, waiting for us? My head jerked left and right, checking to see if anyone was lurking in the shadows. I caught Eddie's eye, pleading to him to tell me what we should do. His face had become an almost greenish colour, as if he was ready to puke. There was no way he was going anywhere near Hazel. He couldn't even look in her direction without gagging. Hazel needed our help. I guess it was up to me to check if she was okay.

'Tess, please,' Hazel pleaded.

Taking a huge breath, I took a step towards her. I trudged my way to the stairs and stepped over the fire extinguisher, almost retching when I saw it was covered in Hazel's blood. My legs were stiff, refusing to bend, like I was wearing brand new batting pads, as I climbed the stairs one at a time.

Kneeling next to her, my eyes immediately fell on the huge gash on her head. I looked away, swallowing my sick back down. She looked nothing like a horrible thief anymore. Instead, she looked defeated, and almost dead.

I felt sorry for her. No one deserved to be attacked and hurt this badly.

'Are you okay?' I asked, then immediately regretted it. This was worse than asking someone if they were okay when they'd just been bowled for a golden duck. Of course she wasn't okay. 'Whooohooohoo did this to you?'

'Him.' Her voice was raspy, and she was breathing heavily.

'Him? Him who?' I asked.

'He tricked me.'

'Do you mean the man you stole the Urn for?' Hazel gave a slight nod, then winced at the pain. 'What's his name?'

'Don't know. Can't remember.'

Don't know? I thought. How could she still not know who this dangerous lunatic was?

'Where's the Urn? Did he take it?'

'Yes.'

Dang it! What were we supposed to do now? I wanted to ask her more questions about who this man was and where he might have taken the Urn, but she looked so awful, and we had to get her help. It was obvious that even though she was the one who had actually stolen the Urn from Lord's, she was also a victim. Hazel wasn't to blame. The mastermind behind this whole plan was to blame. We just didn't know who he was.

'Hazel, we'll call you an ambulance and get you some help. Do you know the way out of here?'

117

Hazel nodded and pointed to the door behind her. Thank goodness! Finally, a way out of this underground nightmare.

'Okay, good. Just lay still.'

Again, Hazel gave the slightest of nods. 'You need to get it back.'

'We will, I promise.'

She closed her eyes. I knew we should get her to a hospital, but I also really needed to find out as much as I could before she was taken away. I had to know who the man was. I glanced down at Eddie, who was still rooted to the spot. I pointed at his phone. He understood and held it in the air looking for service, happy to have something to distract him. I reached into my pocket and pulled out the few remaining tissues I had left. Folding them into a wad, I pressed them against Hazel's head wound.

'I need your socks,' I called down to Eddie. He looked puzzled. 'To use as a bandage.'

'Oh, okay, but they aren't very clean.'

'They'll be okay.' I grinned. When had Eddie ever cared about clean socks?

Eddie put his phone down and took off his socks. Throwing them to me, I stretched them as much as I could, then tied them together. Wrapping them around Hazel's head, I tucked the tops into each other. It wasn't perfect, but it would do the job.

'Any luck?' I called out to Eddie.

'Not yet. Does Hazel know where we are?'

Hazel heard him, and answered, 'Hotel.'

'Which hotel, Hazel?'

'Can't remember.'

Dang it! She must have concussion.

I ran down to Eddie. His face still had a greenish tinge, although, thank goodness, it didn't look as though he was going to be sick anymore.

'What's happening?' he asked.

'It's a bit of a jumble as I think she's got concussion. She's got a huge gash on her head. But she says she was tricked into stealing the Urn. She can't remember his name but he's the one who also attacked her.'

'That's messed up. Is she going to be okay?'

'I don't know, we need to get her to a hospital. She says the way out is through those doors. Do you want to go and try and get a signal and I'll wait here?'

'No, I'm not leaving you behind.'

'Eddie, I'll be fine. I need to find out who the man is and where he's taken the Urn.'

'No – what if the man comes back?'

That made me stop and think. I shook my head. 'I doubt he's going to come back here; he has the Urn and that's all he wanted.'

'Doesn't matter. I'm not leaving you.'

I loved Eddie for being so loyal. He was right, we couldn't split up. But I couldn't let this go. 'Okay, give me two minutes to speak to Hazel again and then we'll both go.'

'Fine. Two minutes. That's all!'

Hazel still looked pale, but no blood was seeping through the temporary sock bandage.

'Hazel, we're going to have to go outside to call an ambulance and the police. You need to tell me as much about him as you can. What was inside the Urn that he wanted so badly?'

Between raspy breaths, Hazel explained the best she could. 'Nothing in the Urn but the original ashes … Tricked me … All a lie … Never going to let me keep it …' She closed her eyes in pain. I needed more, so I gently shook her shoulder. Her eyes flickered open and shut. 'Where's my phone? … Took picture.'

I looked back at the cracked phone and sighed. Dang it! I crossed all my fingers and toes as I bounded down the stairs and picked it up. Eddie was still waving his arm in the air to get a signal and he shook his head. Pressing the home key, I nearly cheered when the locked screen appeared through the cracks.

'Tess, your two minutes are up,' Eddie said, and I heard the warning in his voice.

'Okay, okay. She still doesn't know his name, but she said there's a picture of him on her phone. I'll just get her to open it and we'll be able to see who he is.'

Eddied stepped in front of me, blocking my way. 'She still doesn't know his name? This whole thing is ridiculous.'

'I know, but if we have a photo of him, we'll be able to

track him down.'

'And then what?'

'Then we'll go find him and get the Urn back.'

'Tess, are you crazy? You can see what he did to Hazel, and she was the one who was doing all the dirty work for him. Imagine what he'd do to two interfering kids like us. Now's the time to call the police and tell them everything we know.'

I paused for a second and thought about what Eddie had said. He was right, of course, but he'd been taking risks all day without listening to me, so why did he get to decide what was too risky?

'How is it any riskier than crossing the train tracks?'

Eddie recoiled from my spiteful words. 'That's not fair!'

I winced, I knew it was a low blow, but I refused to back down. 'Maybe, but we're so close to finding the final puzzle piece and I think we should go for it.'

'But Tess, I almost died, and we were locked in that room and left to die. Holy Moly, I almost died twice in the one day! It's way too serious now, we need to call the police.'

I shuddered as the image of rats demolishing the sandwich flashed before my eyes. I turned to look at Hazel's bashed head. I sighed and dropped my shoulders. Eddie was right. We'd reached the point where we needed help.

'Okay, fine. But can we at least look at the photo first?

I'm dying to know who it is.' Eddie gave me a sideways look and I rolled my eyes. 'Okay, maybe "dying" wasn't the best choice of words. But what if we recognise him? We'll be able to tell the police who it is.'

Eddie grinned. 'Fine, but as soon as Hazel shows you the photo we get out of here and call the police.'

Nodding, I ran up the stairs to Hazel's side again and held the phone up for her to unlock. I tried not to look at the bloody fingerprint she left on the screen. All that mattered was that the phone was now unlocked.

'That's him,' Hazel mumbled. 'Find him. I'm sorry.'

A tear slid down her cheek as she closed her eyes. All the anger I had towards her disappeared and turned towards this horrid man who had tricked Hazel in the most despicable way. Totally forgetting I'd promised Eddie only seconds earlier that we'd call the police, all I wanted to do was to find him and make him pay. And, of course, get the Urn back to Lord's.

Wiping the blood off with Hazel's sleeve, I squinted at the picture through the cracks. I could see a man in a suit, with his back turned as if he was walking away. His head was cut off, so it was impossible to tell who it was. If this was the only evidence Hazel had, we were at a dead end. I sat on the step next to her and shook my head at Eddie. This was it: whoever it was really had gotten away with it. I felt awful, like I'd let everyone down. Once again, we were so close to finding out the truth and saving cricket only to have it snatched away. All we could do now was call Dad or the police and face the consequences.

Hazel reached out and pulled me close. 'He was so angry that I messed everything up. I understand now. The Urn doesn't belong to me, you need to get it back. But I didn't tell him you were here. He doesn't know about you.'

As I laid the phone next to Hazel, my eyes fell to the man's shoes. They were so shiny that the light from the flash had reflected off them as bright as a Zing Bail flying off the stumps. I leapt up. I knew exactly where I'd seen them before and exactly who this man was.

16

THE TOSS

The two captains flip a coin at the start of a match, with the winner choosing whether to bat or bowl

'I know who it is!' I shouted at Eddie. 'I know who took the Urn.'

'What? How?' Eddie frowned and climbed halfway up the stairs, making sure to keep enough distance between himself and the blood.

'Look at his shoes. Don't you recognise them?' I shoved the phone in Eddie's face.

He squinted, then shrugged. 'Nope!'

'Urgh! They belong to Jasper Bardwell – you know, the man you said sponsors cricket. When we saw him this morning, I remember thinking he was wearing the shiniest shoes I'd ever seen. And this is them, or him, whatever. See how the light from the flash has reflected on them? That would only happen if they were really shiny.'

'Jasper Bardwell? Come on, Tess, they could be anyone's shoes. My dad's always polishing his shoes, so maybe he's the Urn Thief? You can't tell that it's Jasper Bardwell. And besides, why would he want to steal the Urn? He's one of the richest men in London and can have anything he wants.'

I gave Eddie the most withering glare I could muster. I couldn't believe he wasn't taking me seriously. Okay, so I understood where he was coming from: there were lots of polished shoes out there – but I just knew these belonged to Jasper Bardwell, and I also knew how to prove it was him.

'Eddie, I know you don't believe me. But what if I can prove it? Have you got any data left on your phone?'

His eyes lit up as he checked his phone. 'Better! I'm picking up a small wi-fi signal.' He climbed the last few stairs to stand next to me. 'That should be enough. What do you want me to search?'

'I was thinking if we can get a picture of Jasper and show Hazel, she'll be able to tell me if I'm right.'

Eddie thought about it for a moment. 'Great idea, but if

she doesn't recognise him, do you promise we'll call the police and your dad?'

I paused for only a nanosecond before agreeing. I was certain I was right. Eddie tapped away at his phone then passed it to me. Jasper Bardwell's horrid face smirked back at me, and I swear I could see evil behind his fake smile.

Gently, I tapped Hazel on the shoulder. 'Hazel, wake up. It's me, Tess. Are you able to open your eyes for a minute? We need you to look at a photo, please?'

Hazel stirred a little and groaned. She really needed medical help, but hopefully she was still conscious enough to look at a picture. I held the phone above her face. Her eyes widened. 'That's him,' she said in barely a whisper.

Triumphant, I turned at Eddie and grinned. He gave me a sheepish look in return.

'Now what?' he asked.

I bent back down to Hazel and whispered in her ear. 'Hazel, thank you. We're going to get you some help and we'll make sure everyone knows you were tricked, okay?'

Hazel nodded slightly in acknowledgement. I turned to Eddie. 'Now we get out of these tunnels.'

I grinned as I turned the door handle and it opened with ease. We shielded our eyes as brilliant sunlight flooded in. I couldn't believe the outside world had literally been on the other side of this door. I thought we would have more tunnels or something to navigate before we made it outside. Blinking, I tried to get my bearings. I had no idea how far we'd walked, nor in what direction, so I was surprised to see we were at the hotel opposite the stone frieze where we'd had our photo taken this morning. St John's Wood Road was full of police cars. There was even a helicopter circling overhead. This changed everything; all we had to do was run across the road and get Dad, tell him the whole story and leave it to the police. But something stopped me. I wasn't ready to share it with anyone yet. I wanted Eddie and I to find Jasper and get the Urn back. I motioned for Eddie to step behind the building, out of sight.

'I don't believe it,' he said, for once bewildered by his lack of bearings. 'We're literally back where we started.'

His phone pinged a million times as it found a signal. 'They're from my dad. Your dad must've told him we were missing. They're gonna be so mad. Come on, let's go.' He started to walk away, but I held my ground. He sensed I wasn't following him and turned to me. 'Tess, come *on*,' he pleaded.

'No.' I stomped my foot and Eddie's face clouded over. 'No?'

'No! You literally just agreed we'd go after Jasper if Hazel recognised him.'

'No, I didn't.' Eddie stood his ground, as stubborn as me.

'Yes, you did.'

'No, I made you promise that if she didn't recognise

him, we'd call your dad.'

I threw my hands up in exasperation. 'That's totally the same thing.'

'No, it isn't.'

'Come on, Eddie. We can't give up now.'

Eddie studied the Lord's stone carving across the road where we'd stopped for a photo this morning. How could we have ever known we were about to go on an incredible adventure? I could see that Eddie was weighing everything up in his head. But I couldn't wait any longer. I was sick of him taking all the risks and me following behind.

'Well, I'm going whether you're coming or not.' I turned away and walked in the opposite direction to Lord's.

'He's dangerous, Tess,' Eddie said, stopping me in my tracks. 'He's been manipulating Hazel for months. He's obviously a man who gets what he wants and doesn't care who stands in his way.'

I turned and pleaded with Eddie. 'Jasper doesn't know about us.'

'That doesn't make him any less dangerous.'

'I know, but if we can actually catch him red-handed then I absolutely promise we'll call for help.' I crossed my heart to emphasise just how serious my promise was.

Eddie sighed, then dialled for an ambulance.

'Ambulance is on its way.' His phone rang and he looked at the screen. 'It's Dad, for the millionth time.'

'Are you gonna answer it?' I asked, holding my breath. He let it ring.

'I know where Jasper Bardwell lives.'

Whatever I thought Eddie was going to say, it wasn't that. 'What? How?'

'I saw his address on a letter when we were in Harvey's office.'

'Oh!' I could almost hug him.

Eddie's phone stopped ringing. 'We've got two choices and we better decide quick, as Dad's not going to stop calling me and he'll track my phone as well.'

I nodded.

'So, I'm thinking we toss a coin. Heads we go after Jasper, tails we go back to Lord's. What do you think?'

'Let fate decide? Agreed!'

Eddie retrieved a pound coin from his pocket. 'Ready?' He asked, and I grinned and shouted, 'Heads,' confident the coin would fall my way.

He tossed the coin high into the air. His phone rang again as the helicopter did another circle over Lord's and an ambulance's siren wailed, getting closer and closer. I watched the coin tumbling in the air just like I'd watched the Urn do only hours ago. Two random objects tumbling, both deciding my fate. The coin dropped to the ground then bounced a couple of times before spinning flat. Our heads bumped as we peered over it.

17

THE CHASE

*The last innings of a match where the batting team needs to
score more runs than their opposition to win*

Heads!

Yes! I made a little victory fist. Eddie made an
undecipherable noise next to me. It didn't matter, we were
going to find the Urn.

'Let's go,' I cried and strode off.

'Hang on, Tess, do you even know where you're
going?'

'Well, you said you know where he lives, so that's where we're going, isn't it?' I replied, eager to move on.

'Yeah, I do. But what if he hasn't gone there? Maybe he went back to his office instead?'

This statement stopped me in my tracks. Of course, just because Eddie saw his address on a letterhead didn't mean he went straight home. 'Do you know where his office is?'

'No. So we have to be sure before we just run off.'

'You're right, of course. Can we call his office and ask to speak to him? If they say he's not there, then we can assume he's gone home, can't we?'

'That might work. I just don't have much battery left, and I need to turn it off before Dad rings again.' On cue, Eddie's phone rang, and the wail of the approaching ambulance grew closer. He pulled a face before tapping the reject button and searching for Jasper's work number.

I tried not to giggle as Eddie mimicked his dad's voice. 'Good morning, please may I speak to Jasper Bardwell … Oh, he's not in the office today … Right … No, no need to leave a message … Yes, thank you.'

'There you go!' I beamed. 'So, where does he live?

'Hampstead, so we'll need to catch a train,' Eddie said, shivering at the thought of going near a train. 'Do you have your ticket?'

'Oh no, Dad's got it,' I replied. 'Wait! I've got the money that Grandpa gave me. We could use that?'

'Perfect.'

'Eddie.'

He heard the sharpness in my voice and snapped his head up. 'What?'

'Turn your phone off. We've got to go. *Now*.'

I yanked Eddie's arm and pulled him away from Lord's.

'Tess, what are you doing. What's going on?'

Eddie's face went white as he glanced over his shoulder. Dad, Harvey, and a police officer were running down St John's Wood Road towards us.

'Did they see us?' Eddie said as he frantically turned his phone off.

'I hope not.'

We ran as fast as we could away from the approaching ambulance, Lord's, the police, and my very angry dad, only stopping when we reached Baker Street Station, where we jumped on the first train.

My heart finally returned to normal once we exited Hampstead Station. The sky had clouded over in the time it had taken us to ride the few stops, and it was threatening rain. Maybe the weather people had been right all along.

'I'm hungry,' Eddie declared. It was the first thing either of us had said since we'd run away from Lord's.

'Me too. I've still got some money.'

A police car came wailing down the road, lights flashing. We ducked into the nearest café and watched it drive past. I looked at Eddie and he shook his head. It couldn't be looking for us; police cars were always dashing around London.

After a quick toilet break, where I washed my filthy hands and face the best I could, we ordered some food to go. As we waited, the television on the wall switched from an advert to the news. A reporter stood outside Lord's, and I could see the helicopter whirring in the sky above him. I couldn't hear what he was saying but the captions said there had been an incident at Lord's and the police would be making a statement shortly.

I jabbed Eddie in his ribs as our faces appeared on the screen with the word 'MISSING' in big, bold, red letters underneath. Eddie sucked in his breath, causing the lady behind the counter to give us a sideways look as she handed over our food, although I suddenly wasn't hungry anymore. Grabbing it, we strode out of the café with our heads down so no one would recognise us.

'This way,' Eddie whispered. Thank goodness he'd memorised the map hanging on the station wall and knew exactly where we were going.

Keeping our heads lowered, we stopped a few streets from the station.

'Eddie, our faces are on TV. You don't think they think we had anything to do with stealing the Urn, do you?'

Eddie thought about what I said before he answered. 'No, they're just trying to find us. That's all.'

'Are you sure?'

'I'm sure.'

He might be sure we weren't suspects but having my face on the news made me very nervous. Luckily, there

weren't too many people about now we'd left the main street. Still, every time a car drove past, Eddie and I dropped our heads and turned away. If someone saw us and called the police, we were goners.

I nibbled at my sandwich in silence, not really tasting it, and tried to digest all that had happened. It had been, without a doubt, the most interesting and best and fun and scariest day of my life. Putting words and sentences onto paper usually came easily to me, but today I didn't even know where to start with trying to make sense of everything that had happened. Nevertheless, my fingers were itching to write something, anything, down. Next to me, Eddie had gobbled down his food and shoved his hands in his pockets. He kicked a stone that was on the path. We hadn't spoken for ages, and I was beginning to wonder if he was angry that I'd pushed him into going to Jasper's house.

'Eddie, are you okay? Are you mad at me or something?' I whispered.

He sighed. 'No, not mad, just – I don't know, really. I'm trying to work it all out in my head.'

'I know what you mean. Our parents must be so worried about us.' Eddie didn't answer. 'Should we call them now and let them know we're okay?'

'I thought I was being so clever this morning,' Eddie continued, ignoring my question. 'You know: working out the Urn was a fake, I thought it would be so cool to be a detective, not really thinking we'd actually catch the thief. And we have been amazing detectives, figuring it all out. But I nearly died, twice! Hazel nearly died, our faces are on the news, and now we're on our way to this madman's house. I'm not sure if we're really brave or really stupid?'

I grinned and bumped Eddie's shoulder with mine. 'Yeah, me neither. All I know is I've got this feeling that we're the only ones who can get the Urn back. I know it sounds stupid.'

'It doesn't sound stupid.' Eddie bumped me back. 'I feel the same way. I can't even think about how worried and angry our parents are right now. We've come this far so we might as well see it through and face the consequences later.'

A car approached and slowed down as if they had recognised us. Panicking, I took Eddie's hand. 'Come on, let's go find Jasper's house.'

Jasper's street was wide and tree-lined, and while I knew Jasper was rich, these houses were insane.

'Wowsers!' I exclaimed, and Eddie whistled. 'What number are we looking for?'

'Eighty-three.'

I spotted the number first, screwed into a brick wall next to a metal electric gate. Over the top of the gate, if I stood on tiptoes, I could just see a slate roof; however, the rest of the house was obscured by a hedge and clump of trees.

'We might be able to squeeze through the space

between the hedge and the gate?' Eddie suggested.

I shook my head. 'It's too tight and anyone could see us do that. We need to find another way in.' I scanned along the hedge to where an identical wooden gate marked the other side of the property. There didn't seem to be an easy way in.

'Just great,' I exclaimed, throwing my hands in the air. 'What do we do now?'

'Maybe there's another entrance round the back.' Eddie replied, then grabbed my arm and hissed in my ear. 'That's Jasper's car.'

Driving down the road was a sleek, black, and very expensive-looking car. The windows were blacked-out, making it impossible to see who was driving it. I couldn't understand why Eddie thought it belonged to Jasper, until I saw the number plate:

JB BANK

'What do we do?' I hissed back. 'What if he recognises us from this morning?'

The wooden gate in front of us began to slide open and the car's indicator flashed on. After the car passed through the gate, Eddie tugged on my arm and dragged me down, so we were doubled over. He pulled me behind the car, through the gate and into the trees. Falling to our knees, we crawled as far forward as we could. Pulling back some branches, we watched the car pull up outside the front of the house. Jasper Bardwell stepped from the driver's seat then walked around to the passenger side. He briefly ducked out of sight before re-emerging with a small black bag in his hands. It was the perfect size and shape to hold the Urn.

The smug grin on Jasper's face made my blood boil as he turned and skipped up the steps and through the front door. Hatred rushed through me. He'd tricked Hazel into the stealing the Urn, attacked her, and tried to ruin cricket. What a horrid, horrible man he was. And he obviously thought he'd gotten away with it. He just hadn't counted on Eddie and I figuring it all out. He'd pushed past us this morning and almost run over us just now. He was so blinded by his own greed and self-importance that he couldn't see the kid-detectives that were right in front of him.

18

FOLLOW-ON

In a Test Match, a team can be asked to bat again if they score at least 200 runs fewer in their first innings than the team that batted first

From the front, Jasper's house resembled a giant red doll's house, and I wished I could reach out and open the front so I could see what was going on inside. Instead, we stayed crouched in the bushes while watching all the windows carefully. Every now and then a movement caught my eye, but it was impossible to tell where exactly in the house Jasper was, or if anyone else was in there too.

We would have to go closer.

'There's a security alarm sign on the wall,' Eddie whispered, pointing to the top right corner of the house. 'Can you see any cameras or anything?'

I looked over the outside of the house and back towards the gate we'd come through and couldn't see anything.

'I don't think so.'

'No, me neither,' Eddie replied. 'There was one on the front gate, but it must just be the inside that's alarmed. We should be safe.'

I tapped Eddie's shoulder and pointed to the two large potted plants either side of the front door. Understanding, Eddie gave me the thumbs-up, so we dashed forwards. Our feet crunched over the gravel loud enough to scare some birds in a nearby tree, but hopefully not to be heard from inside the house. Crouching behind the potted plants, I peeked through the thin window beside the front door. The entrance hall was jaw-dropping and had to be bigger than the entire downstairs of my house. My eyes moved up the huge stone staircase to the first floor. A movement in the kitchen doorway caught my eye and I ducked down as Jasper came through and strode across the hall. If he came out the front door we'd be caught red-handed. His shiny shoes clicked across the hall, past the front door, and, thankfully, a door opened and shut to my right. We'd dodged a bouncer, that was sure. Without waiting to see where Jasper went next, Eddie and I snuck out from behind the pots and, pressing ourselves against the wall, followed it around to the back, ducking under the windows as we went.

We both gasped at the exact same moment and came to a dead halt. I totally could not believe what I was seeing. Beyond a white picket fence, the entire garden was a gently sloping lawn, mowed to perfection and ringed by a white rope. In the middle was a cricket pitch, complete with stumps and bails. In the far corner of the garden stood a scoreboard and clock tower with the Old Father Time weathervane sitting on top. To our right was a terrace lined with white benches. It was as if we'd literally been transported back to Lord's, or a miniature version of it. I mean, even the colour of the bricks on the back of the house were the bacon-red of those at the Pavilion. I shuddered.

'Tess, this is really weird,' Eddie whispered.

'I know, right? But just because he's got a creepy obsession with Lord's doesn't prove he took the Urn. We still need solid evidence before we can call the police.'

'Okay, fine, but I have a really strange feeling about this.'

I couldn't believe Eddie was being so cautious. Weird or not, I was really excited.

'Me too, but I just know the Urn is here. Come on, we'll be fine. We're here now so we might as well look through some windows and see if we can see where he's put it.'

We dropped to our knees and crawled between the benches, peeking through the windows as we went. Most of the back half of the house was taken up by a huge open-plan kitchen, dining table and seating area. Apart from the furniture and a big TV on one wall, there was nothing else. No paintings or books. Not even a toaster or kettle on the kitchen worktops.

'Do you actually think he lives here?' Eddie asked.

'I don't know. It's very clean and tidy and I can't see photos of any of his family or friends. But if he does then it's pretty depressing. I mean, he must be really lonely.'

Eddie gave me a sideways look and I shook my head to erase any sympathy I was feeling. 'But that still doesn't mean it's okay to steal or trick or hurt other people,' I added.

'No, it doesn't. Come on, let's see what's through the last window.'

I was bowled over by the last room. Completely different to all the others, it was so full of life, with crammed bookshelves, photos and other precious objects. It was the only evidence that he actually lived here. Again, I felt a tiny ping of sympathy for him; work seemed to be the only thing he lived for.

Jasper sat behind a big mahogany desk, typing on his computer. The little black bag we'd seen him take from his car lay next to him on the desk. When he finished typing, he picked the bag up and disappeared out the door. Eddie crawled back to the kitchen windows, following him.

'He's gone upstairs,' he whispered as loudly as he

could.

'Let's wait a few minutes and see what he does next,' I replied.

My knees were hurting from kneeling on the concrete ground, but I didn't dare move in case Jasper was looking out of an upstairs window and could see me. After what felt like an eternity, Eddie finally had some news.

'He's coming back down, and it doesn't look like he's got the bag anymore.'

Right, so he must have left it upstairs somewhere. That's where we needed to go next. I had started to crawl across to Eddie when he made a sudden movement and fell flat on the ground. One look at his face made my own heart beat wildly, and I dropped to the ground too. Eddie slid under a bench as the patio doors swung open. As slowly as possible, I pressed my belly into the concrete ground and slid under the nearest bench. As if the bench was going to give me any protection. The seats were made of slats. All Jasper had to do was look down and he'd see us. That was if he didn't hear my thumping heart first.

Paralysed with fear, my eyes followed two shiny shoes as they passed within inches of my nose before stopping at the gate. Jasper puffed out his chest and raised his arms above his head in victory. On cue, the clouds let out an almighty boom as lightning seared through the sky. Jasper laughed. My stomach turned in disgust. I couldn't wait to see the smug smile wiped from his face when he realised two children had caught him.

The hugest bumblebee I'd ever seen came buzzing towards me. Just my luck, it stopped and hovered right above my nose. I desperately wanted to brush it away but knew that even the slightest movement would alert Jasper to my already precarious hiding spot. Instead, I blew at it lightly, hoping to scare it enough to encourage it to move on. It didn't, and buzzed even closer. I risked a peek at Eddie, who shook his head slightly. Holding my breath, I scrunched my eyes shut and forced my hands to stay by my sides, trying to convince myself the bumblebee was after a beautiful-smelling flower and not a rat poo-smelling girl. I never knew how loud a bumblebee's buzz could be as it buzzed around my ears. *Please don't sting me, please don't sting me*, I begged, trying hard not to sob out loud. Eventually, it gave up and flew away to find something more appealing. I exhaled as quietly as I could, more relieved than when the umpire shouts 'not out' after you get hit on the pads.

I unscrewed my eyes in time to see Jasper turn around and go back into the house, so engrossed in his own self-importance that he couldn't see two Cricket Detectives right under his nose. Only when I heard the click of his shiny shoes on the floor fade away, and the study door close, did I exhale another breath. And only when I heard his voice through the study window did my body relax.

'Let's go,' Eddie hissed as he extracted himself and disappeared through the kitchen doors before I could reply. My heart was still pounding as I followed him, more determined than ever to wipe the smile off Jasper's arrogant face.

Tiptoeing through the kitchen to the entrance hall, we kept one eye on the study door as we climbed the staircase. The longest corridor I'd ever seen ran along the first floor, where a number of open doors revealed bedrooms with a bed, side tables, and nothing else. Even Jasper's bedroom looked like it was hardly used. The bed was perfectly made, with no crinkles or creases. I wished I could make my bed that well. On the dresser was a single photo of a boy in cricket whites. Was that Jasper? Did he used to play cricket?

There was only one closed door in the entire corridor. And beside it was a security pad. This had to be where he'd put the Urn.

'What do you reckon the code is?' I asked.

'Dunno,' Eddie replied as he studied the keypad. 'And I'm not sure how many chances we'll get before we get locked out or it sets off an alarm.'

Below us, we heard the creak of the study door and the click of Jasper's shiny shoes. We jumped into the nearest bedroom and hid behind the bed. The room was immaculate; the bed was so perfectly made that I doubted that Jasper had ever had any guests here to sleep in it. My heart, only having just recovered, beat erratically once more. I wasn't sure how much more it could take. A toilet flushed before Jasper returned once more to the study.

'We need some sort of powder or something to dust for

fingerprints on the keypad,' I said. 'That's what all great detectives would do.'

'Hmm,' he agreed. 'I'm not sure we'll find anything like that here. I think our only option is to work out what the code is.'

'So, let's think about this logically. He's obsessed with cricket, even if it's for the wrong reasons, so maybe the passcode is something to do with cricket?'

'That's a great idea, but it literally could be anything. Cricket is full of statistics and scores and dates. How do we narrow it down?'

Eddie was right. It could be anything from 99.94, Don Bradman's Test average, or 8/34, Botham's best bowling figures, or any date in cricket history. The only thing I could be certain of was that it had to be something to do with The Ashes. That was it! It was so obvious. Except I couldn't remember the exact date. Eddie would, though.

'Eddie, what was the date The Ashes started? You know, when English cricket died?'

'Oh yes! Tess, you're a genius.'

I watched as Eddie typed 29081882 into the keypad. Nothing happened. He tried again, this time using the abbreviated year: 290882. The light turned green, and the door unlocked.

19

STUMPED

A way of getting a batter out if, after a legal delivery, the wicketkeeper knocks the bails off with the ball and the batter is out of their crease

The door swung open to reveal a small flight of stairs leading up to two white doors. Beyond the doors was a huge room that extended the entire width of the house. To our left were white-framed, floor-to-ceiling windows with a row of high-backed chairs facing out. The other three walls were light blue and covered with paintings, while two wooden fireplaces were on the back wall. Three enormous chandeliers twinkled from the ceiling. I blinked my eyes, again scarcely able to believe what I was seeing. Although we'd only had a quick glimpse earlier today through the exact same doors I was peering through now, I knew with absolute certainty that this attic room was a replica of the Long Room.

Running the length of the room were two rows of glass cabinets crammed with cricket memorabilia. Had it all been stolen too? I shook my head in disbelief. How could Jasper's obsession have gone so far without anyone noticing?

A spotlight shone from the ceiling, drawing our eyes to a pedestal in the centre of the room. On top of it sat the Urn, basking in the limelight, as if it literally had no idea of the huge adventure it had just been on. The Urn looked so tiny in this huge room, I suddenly felt in awe of its presence. There couldn't be any doubts that it belonged at Lord's, the Home of Cricket, so it could inspire anyone who saw it.

'Thank goodness,' I said, feeling both elation and relief sweep through my body. We'd found it. We'd actually found the Urn and saved cricket.

Pushing open the doors, Eddie ran over to the pedestal with a huge grin on his face, while I bounced along behind him. I was so proud of us. We could have easily given up at any stage today, and there had been many times we probably should have. Nevertheless, we'd followed our instincts, backed each other, and now we had the Urn, and

its thief, in our grasp. Jasper had been so close to getting away with his despicable crime and denying the cricket world this most treasured prize.

'Do we just take it?' I asked.

'I don't know,' Eddie replied unhelpfully.

'So, what do we do?'

Eddie walked to one of the glass cabinets and began examining the door and all the edges. 'It doesn't look like there's a lock on the doors, so maybe there aren't any alarms either? Which makes sense, as I doubt anyone else even knows this room even exists.'

'So, we can just take it and run?' I said, again. 'Or call the police?'

Eddie shook his head, confusing me. 'Maybe not: Jasper is far too dangerous. We've got all the proof we need that he's the thief, so I think we should take a photo of it, call the police, and wait for them to get here. The Urn isn't going anywhere, and Jasper can't know that we're here and we've found it. You know what he did to Hazel.'

I remembered Hazel's bloodied face and shuddered. 'Okay, that sounds more like a plan.'

Eddie reached into his pocket to retrieve his phone. The phone was wedged in, and he yanked it hard. His elbow banged into a glass cabinet with a thud. We both watched in horror as a bat inside the cabinet wobbled before falling sideways. The sound echoed around the room as it smashed into the glass base, shattering it. Tiny cracks slowly began to spread out, making the glass look worse than a fifth-day wicket. Moments later, an alarm rang out, piercing our ear drums.

'We have to get out of here, *now*,' Eddie shouted.

I reached for the Urn.

'No, leave it.' Eddie grabbed my arm and dragged me away.

'I can't leave it behind!'

'You have to, Jasper can't know we're here. He has to think the bat fell by itself. All we can do now is get out and call the police.'

'But –'

'No buts, we have to go.'

He was right. But still, I hopped from foot to foot, my arm dangling as close to the Urn as I dared.

'Tess, leave it.'

The alarm wailed and I was conscious of the seconds ticking by. It took all my effort to leave the Urn behind as I reluctantly scampered after Eddie towards the staircase. We were too late, as we heard the chime from the security pad being pressed on the other side of the door. Oh no! Skidding to halt, we had no choice than to turn around and back-track to the fake Long Room. Standing in the middle of the room, we searched desperately for a hiding place.

'The far fireplace,' I hissed. We sprinted and ducked underneath the mantelpiece just as Jasper burst through the door. It wasn't a real fireplace, so it had no chimney, and Eddie and I found ourselves squeezing into yet another cramped space. Peering over Eddie's knees, I could see Jasper through a gap between two of the cabinets. If I could see him, that meant he could see me too.

Jasper punched some numbers into a panel near the door and, instantaneously, the alarm stopped ringing. He crossed to the damaged cabinet, meaning we were out of his line of sight. He inspected the outside with a puzzled expression before opening the door and picking up the bat. He immediately swore and dropped it again. Blood formed on his fingertip as he shoved it in his mouth. As he sucked his finger, he surveyed the rest of the room. His face grew even more confused, as he couldn't see anything else out of place, nor, extraordinarily, Eddie and I hiding in the fireplace. His phone rang, startling us, and I jumped, bumping my head. Eddie glared at me, so I bit my lip to stop from crying out.

'Hello … Yes, this is he … Appears to be a false alarm … Yes, something fell and triggered it … No, no need to send anyone out … Yes, I'll change that. Thank you.'

With one last sweeping look of bewilderment, Jasper strode out of the fake Long Room. We tumbled out of the fireplace. I rubbed the bump on my head while Eddie stretched his long legs out and shook them. He protested as I tried to pull him to his feet.

'My legs are cramped. I need a minute.'

'We haven't got a minute.'

'I know … Okay.' Eddie groaned again as he forced

himself up.

I ran as Eddie hobbled across the fake Long Room and down the stairs. I tapped in the code. Nothing happened. I tapped again. Still nothing.

'He must have changed the code,' Eddie said, still shaking the pins and needles out of his legs.

'Yes, but to what?'

'I don't know. We need to call our dads and the police.' I nodded and tapped my foot impatiently, waiting for Eddie to turn his phone on. Before he could dial, his phone starting ringing. Eddie pressed the green button before it made any more noise.

'Dad? Dang it!' he hissed, then almost threw his phone on the floor. 'It's dead.'

Noooo! We were going to be dead too if we couldn't find a way out of here. We had to work out what the new code was, and fast. Frantically, Eddie tapped in any random cricket statistic he could think of.

341 Ashes Tests – Red light.

903/7 Highest Ashes Innings – Red light.

1932-33 Bodyline Series – Red light.

124.8 grams, the weight of the Urn – Red light.

Red light.

Red light.

Red light.

We were stumped.

20

CAUGHT

A way of getting a batter out if a fielder catches the ball before it touches the ground after the batter hits it with either their bat or glove

'It's no good!' Eddie said. 'It literally could be anything. We just got lucky last time.'

'Argh! We'll have to find another way out.' I bounded back up the stairs, my eyes darting left and right, up and down, trying to find another exit. Our only option was the windows. I ran to the nearest one and looked out. The storm had built up even farther, and bulbous black clouds now surrounded the mini-Lord's Cricket Ground. Trees swayed in the wind, like a Mexican wave. I gulped. Standing on tiptoes, I could just see over the slanting roof to the red tiles of a small balcony on the second floor below. I turned to Eddie standing next to me and he nodded. We had to get down to the balcony.

Eddie unfastened the locks and gripped the lower sash. He pulled as hard as he could, but it didn't budge. Gritting his teeth, he tried again. It still didn't budge. He let go and leaned his forehead on the glass. 'It's too heavy.'

'I'll help.' I dragged one of the tall chairs over and scrambled on top of the seat. Standing on tiptoes, I stretched my body as long as it could go, and felt my fingers only just reach the top sash. 'On the count of three.'

My tiny muscles burned as I pushed up as hard as I could. Inch by inch, the window began to rise. Eddie slid his hands into the gap to get a better grip, and the window suddenly gained traction, slipping up and out of my fingers. The wind slapped into me, making my eyes water and my legs wobble. Frantically, I reached my arms out for something to grasp to stop myself falling through the open window and rolling down the roof and straight over the edge.

'I've got you, Tess.' I felt Eddie's arms fasten around my legs, anchoring me. My clawing fingers brushed the sides of the window and I clung tight, my life depending on it. Careful not to look down, I focused on Old Father

Time at the end of the garden. He was twisting and turning in the storm, and I was certain he was taking the stumps off, calling our time. Taking a few deep breaths, I waited for my heartbeat to return to normal.

'You okay?' Eddie asked. I took a few more breaths before giving a shaky, 'Yes,' in reply.

'HEY! STOP!' A voice boomed from behind, making me wobble once more and my heart pound so hard I thought it was going to burst right through my chest. Snapping my head towards the voice, I saw Jasper was standing in the doorway with the most shocked expression I'd ever seen. If I hadn't been clinging to an open window in the middle of a storm, I would have laughed. Instead, I froze as his face transformed to a menacing glare. He took a couple of steps towards us.

'Tess, go,' Eddie shouted. He gave me the slightest nudge, but I was already ducking under the sash. I jumped onto the roof, half expecting my feet to slip. However, it wasn't slippery, just steep. Trying to stand, I kept falling forwards, struggling to find my balance. Squatting, I sat on my bottom before resting my hands on the tiles behind me. The howling wind wasn't helping, but I couldn't think about that now. I had to focus on getting down to the balcony. Shuffling a few inches forward, I twisted my head around to warn Eddie to be careful. Except he wasn't at the window. Where was he? Fear knotted inside my belly; what if Jasper had caught him?

I called out. 'Eddie?' As I turned onto my hands and

knees, ready to crawl back, Eddie's face popped out of the window, startling me. I dug my toes into the tiles to prevent myself from sliding.

'Here, Tess, take this,' Eddie shouted as he shoved the Urn in my face. I balked. 'Come on, Tess, take it.'

After everything that had happened today, and all that we'd been through to get the Urn back, I was suddenly too scared to touch it.

'Tess!'

I could hear Jasper shouting and swearing behind Eddie as his heavy feet stomped towards us. I raised my hand and felt the weight of responsibility drop into it. The Urn felt so tiny, but I could almost feel a beat inside it, as if it was alive. This Urn was the heartbeat of cricket and I had to keep it safe.

Eddie began to climb out the window and I had to move, or he'd jump on top of me. Thinking quickly, I pulled my collar open so I could drop the Urn down the front of my tucked-in shirt, knowing it would be safe. My hand was shaking so much as I tried to drop the Urn inside my shirt. Distracted by Eddie about to jump, I looked up for a split second and my hand missed the opening of my shirt. The Urn fell. Crashing my elbows onto the roof, I snatched it millimetres before it hit the tiles. That was too close! I didn't miss the second time and felt the Urn settle between my shirt and belly. A drop of rain landed by my foot, leaving a small dark circle on the roof tile. Then another and another. Seconds later, all the tiles had turned dark and slippery.

Eddie thumped down on the tiles just as Jasper's head and shoulders appeared through the open window. His face was more thunderous than the clouds above. Carefully, but as quickly as possible, I flipped over and shuffled to the roof edge. The drop to the balcony was longer than I thought. Eddie would make the jump easily, but I wasn't so sure I would.

'Stop there, you two little brats, or I'm calling the police,' Jasper shouted. Balancing myself, I looked back. Jasper had poked his head and shoulders out farther until he completely filled the frame, raising my hopes that he might not be able to fit through it.

'Call the police,' Eddie shouted back. 'And tell them you stole the Urn and we're taking it back.'

Jasper flinched before a smug grin crossed his face. 'What do you mean, I stole the Urn? That's a replica and you have no proof otherwise. You're just two filthy little thieves who have broken into my house.'

I really wanted to laugh in his face and tell him just how wrong he was, but my fear of talking to adults crept up and my mouth felt like it was sewn shut.

'We all know it's not a replica,' Eddie shouted.

Jasper's face turned bright red. He thrust one leg over the windowsill, trying to climb out, huffing and puffing as he squeezed his round body through the square hole. Finally, he popped through, gripping the windowsill tight so the momentum of his huge body didn't propel him

forwards.

'It belongs to me, and you had better give it back or I'll push you both over the edge.'

I looked at his fingers turning white under the strain of holding himself up. He couldn't risk letting go, so I was confident he couldn't follow through with his threat. Not that it mattered, as our only way out was the balcony below. Whilst the drop might not kill me, it would definitely hurt and probably break a few bones.

'Push us and the Urn goes too,' Eddie scoffed. I looked at Eddie, baffled as to where he was getting his bravado from. I was terrified. We were trapped on a rooftop with a vicious thief in pursuit. Why couldn't I have even a fraction of his fearlessness? But I did, didn't I? I'd done so many courageous things today that I had never imagined I could do. I knew I could be brave again.

The rain continued to lash as we eyed each other off. Eddie and I were so close to the edge, clinging desperately as each gust of wind smacked into us. Jasper made to lurch at us, but his feet slipped, and he gripped even more tightly. He glared at us with such hatred. I couldn't imagine what had happened to make him so angry. Not defeated, he tried a different tactic, flashing a creepy smile. 'So, tell me. How did you find me?'

'We followed the dirty little trail you left.' Eddie shouted, continuing to taunt Jasper.

'Hazel!' Jasper almost spat out her name. 'I knew I shouldn't have trusted that stupid woman. Ah! Now I remember. I saw you both this morning, didn't I? You were in my way then and you're in my way now. You've seen what I did to Hazel and that's what I'm going to do to you two if you do not give me the Urn back. Now!'

His voice was so spiteful, it caused a chill to run down my spine. Nevertheless, my anger began to rise listening to him. I absolutely refused to hand the Urn over to him. Thank goodness Eddie had thought to grab it. It was our only leverage.

'Why do you want it so badly?' Eddie asked, ignoring Jasper's threats. 'You're so rich you can buy anything you want.'

'That's exactly why, boy: I can buy anything I want – except for the Urn. And if I can't buy something, I just take it.'

'Y-y-y-you horrible, selfish man. Wh-wh-wh-why are you doing this?' I screamed, taking everyone, even myself, by surprise, then immediately shrinking back down under Jasper's menacing glare. Eddie locked eyes with me and gave me a small nod. He had faith in me. I just needed to have faith in myself.

'Why?' he sneered. 'Because of children like you.'

'Like us?' Eddie asked incredulously.

'Not you personally, but children like you. All I ever wanted to do was to play cricket. Every year, no matter how much I trained, everyone laughed at me and teased me. I was always last to bat, last to bowl, and no one cared. I vowed that I'd show them all. And even after I showered everyone with money, I still wasn't part of a team. No one likes me, they just want me for my money. So, I built this house and collected all these things. And I decided I deserved the one thing that money couldn't buy. I spent years working out a plan and you two little punks have ruined it all.'

I heard the pain in Jasper's voice as he told us about how unfairly he'd been treated – actually, not just unfairly treated, but bullied, and for the briefest of moments I felt a solidarity with him. I knew what it was like to be singled out and bullied. It was the worst. I also knew how lucky I was that Eddie had come to my rescue and was now my best friend. If only someone had shown more empathy towards Jasper and made him feel part of a team, then we might not be here today. I needed to tell him that he wasn't alone and maybe he would see sense and just let us give the Urn back. Taking a deep breath, I tried to conjure all the emotions I'd had every time I'd been bullied, to help Jasper overcome his pain.

'Mr Bardwell, I'm so sorry you were bullied. I've been bullied too, but I was lucky that Eddie stood up for me. It's not fair that everyone was so mean to you. If I'd been there, I would have been your friend.'

'Ha!' He spat back at me. 'A girl sticking up for me? I would have been even more ridiculed if a girl had befriended me. Girls don't belong in cricket.'

I gasped, winded, as his spiteful words crashed into me. Eddie tried to grab me, but I slapped his hands away. I no longer felt sorry for Jasper. His very soul had been corrupted by his greed and envy. He hated the world and everyone around him. Life was too short to let horrid people ruin it for you. You either cowered away or stood up to them. He'd chosen his path and now I was choosing mine. Rising to my feet, I balanced precariously on the edge of the roof, ignoring the wind and rain that was plummeting into me. I flicked my plaits over my shoulders and looked Jasper square in the eye. This was my fight, and I was ready.

'It seems to me, Mr Bardwell, that it's you who has the problem and no one else. You have held a grudge all these years and chosen to be the victim. You've manipulated and bullied Hazel into stealing the Urn for yourself. You hate everyone so you can't forgive and move on. And despite what you think, girls *do* belong in cricket. Cricket is for everyone. And the Urn is for everyone. It is a symbol that even the biggest enemies can come together, and it inspires EVERY cricketer from EVERY part of the world. It does not and never will belong to you, and Eddie and I are taking it back.'

21

SLIPS

Fielding positions behind the stumps, next to the wicketkeeper

Jasper recoiled, shocked that a little girl would have the audacity to speak to him like that. As he did, his feet slipped from under him. He scrambled desperately to regain his footing. It didn't work: the rain was now so heavy it was cascading down the tiles and over the edge like a mini waterfall. His bulk dragged him down, his fingers lost their grip on the windowsill, and momentum carried him forwards as he slipped down the roof, giving us only seconds to jump out of the way and avoid being bowled over. Jasper screamed as he rolled over the edge, and I heard a loud thump as he landed on the balcony below.

I peered over the edge. However, the balcony was no longer below me. I'd jumped too far to the right. All I could see through the teeming rain was the bench-covered terrace, two storeys below. Over on the balcony, Jasper lay slumped on the floor. He wasn't moving. Oh no! Had I killed him? He groaned. Thank goodness. Gingerly, he got to his feet and limped through the balcony door.

'Tess!' Eddie shouted. Instinctively, I snapped my head in his direction, making me wobble. Unable to regain my balance, my feet slipped off the roof and onto the gutter. I screamed as a bracket snapped and the gutter bowed. A gust of wind slapped into me. Hearing another crack, I knew it would only be moments before the gutter broke off completely and I fell. Shifting all my momentum forward, I came crashing down onto the tiles, landing heavily on my knees. Pain radiated up my legs, but the only thought I had was to protect the Urn nestled inside my shirt. I flipped onto my back and dug my fingers into the tiles to anchor myself. They were too steep and slippery. In slow-motion, I slid towards to edge. My toes dangled over, then my legs. There was nothing to stop me. I closed my eyes, unable to watch as I fell.

My elbow snapped as Eddie grabbed my hand, jolting me to a stop. The benches blurred beneath my dangling feet and my stomach lurched. The only comfort was that I could see the small bulge of the Urn safe inside my shirt. Looking up, Eddie was flat on his stomach, lying across the roof, and the strain on his face was evident as he gripped my hand while desperately trying to anchor himself and prevent me from dragging him down.

'Tess, I'm going to swing you towards the balcony so you can jump on it. Okay?' he yelled at me.

'Are you crazy?' I screamed back, squirming in fear. 'I'll never make it.'

'Tess, stay still, I can't hold you if you keep moving.'

'Eddie, I'm scared, it's too far.'

'I know, but I can't hold you any longer.' As if to prove his point, our wet palms slipped, and I screamed as Eddie tightened his grip.

'Okay, okay,' I sobbed.

'Okay.'

Like a pendulum, Eddie began to swing me back and forth so that the benches below me became a blur. After each swing, my legs swung closer and closer to the balcony, and I was relieved to see that my feet could nearly touch the railing. Thank goodness for Eddie's long arms.

'Ready?' he shouted, and I nodded.

Taking a deep breath, I steadied myself and focused on the balcony. Timing the jump we both yelled, 'NOW!' at the same time. I felt Eddie's hand release me and I launched myself, flying through the air. The benches

below me disappeared and the red tiles of the balcony came into view. A huge gust of wind propelled me the last few feet, and placing one hand protectively over the Urn, my feet landed on the tiles, sending more jolts of pain through my knees. I bounced forward and completed a somersault landing with a thud on my back, knocking the wind right out of me. Gasping for breath and trying not to choke on rain, I grinned. I'd survived AND I'd saved the Urn. Above me, Eddie cheered. In a flash, his long legs dangled as he lowered himself down, still whooping in triumph.

I closed my eyes as the joyous sound of police sirens came screeching to a halt out the front of Jasper's house.

22

SAFE

The batter is 'safe' when they have completed a run before a fielder can break the stumps with the ball

I smoothed down the skirt on my dress and grinned at Eddie who looked super cool in his suit and tie. Through the window, I scanned the crowd, unable to find a spare seat in any of the stands. The only gaps belonged to where the Bardwell & Co. advertising signs had hastily been removed. Yesterday, seeing all those people would have sent me spiralling into a state of panic, afraid I would get it wrong and that everyone would laugh at me. Today, I didn't have a care in the world. I smiled at Dad, who grinned back at me, pride written all over his face. He placed his hand on my shoulder and gave it a squeeze, causing me to wince. Every part of me ached, but I couldn't care less.

Jack Beaufort, the journalist who had inadvertently played a huge part in yesterday's events, was at the back of the room, snapping photos and jotting down notes. He had been appointed the official reporter for the Test Match, ensuring he landed the scoop of the century, and thanks to him, this morning Eddie and I were on the front page of his, and every other, newspaper.

By the time Jack had told everyone his story – and they'd believed him – we'd already found Hazel and were planning how we could catch Jasper when Eddie's phone had gotten a signal and they tracked us to the hotel opposite Lord's. Although Hazel had been barely conscious when everyone had found her, she'd managed to tell them what had happened before she was whisked to hospital, where she was now recovering. Even though she wasn't the mastermind behind the plan, she was still in a heap of trouble as she'd been the one who'd actually stolen the Urn. Dad told me she was cooperating with the police, telling them how Jasper had orchestrated the whole thing, so he thought she might get off on good behaviour. I think she was just a really vulnerable person, and Jasper had taken advantage of that, and bullied her into stealing the Urn. No one deserved to be manipulated and attacked the way she had been, so I was glad that she wouldn't be punished.

Eddie and I had lain on the balcony giddy with exhaustion and jubilation, listening to the police burst into Jasper's house and arrest him. We'd been really nervous hearing my dad call out to us, not knowing exactly how much trouble we were in. He'd yelled a lot, then hugged us so tightly. He didn't let go while he listened in disbelief as we told him how we'd strung all the clues together. Then he gave us a lecture about how dangerous it had been and how we should have gone to him and told him what we were up to – blah blah blah. But everything was forgiven. We were safe, the Urn was safe, and cricket was safe.

We were treated like heroes when we arrived back at Lord's and returned the Urn to the Museum, and I honestly haven't been able to wipe the smile from my face since. All that mattered was that the Urn was safe and back where it belonged.

Jasper Bardwell confessed to plotting to steal the Urn. I was trying really hard not to feel sorry for him, as he was a horrible man, but I kept going back to when he had told us about his childhood. His life could have been totally different for him if even one person had included him or stood up for him. That's all it took – one person – and that person could change someone's life forever. I looked over to Eddie, grateful that I had that one person as my best friend.

Eddie and I were special guests of the MCC for the first day of the Test today, which meant I had to wear a dress. I actually didn't mind wearing one. Not only was I a proper cricketer, but I was also now officially a proper detective, and detectives should always look their best after they have solved a case. Besides, Harvey said I had to, and Mum would have killed me if I'd even argued one tiny bit.

As a special treat this morning we were allowed to go into the Players' Dressing Rooms and take photos of all the names and finally get to sit in our heroes' seats. Some of the players had even wanted to get their photos with us! It was so cool. We also finally got to go into the *real* Long Room. It was a million times better than the pretend one Jasper had built. The captains were waiting for us and we had our photos taken with them, although not with the Urn as planned, as the chances of it ever coming out from its cabinet any time soon were practically zero.

'So, you two have had a big adventure,' the England Captain had said. Eddie opened his mouth to reply, but I beat him to it.

'We sure have!' I said, and proceeded to tell him everything.

Eddie grinned at me, and I winked at Mum and Dad when I'd seen their shocked faces at my newfound confidence. I didn't need to be scared to talk to anyone anymore. People were only scary if you let them be, and the more you ran away from your fears, or blamed everyone else, the harder it was to defeat them. I didn't wish I could be more like Eddie anymore. Now I was finally happy with being me.

'Okay kids, it's time,' Harvey said as he opened the balcony door. Behind me, Grandpa sat in his wheelchair, grinning from ear to ear. In his hand he held a copy of the Test Match programme, and he had read my story a dozen times already, showing it to anyone who was standing within five feet of him. He gave me a wink. He hadn't been mad when I'd told him I'd spent all the money he'd given me on train tickets and food while we solved the case of the stolen Urn. Instead, he told me he was the proudest Grandpa in the world.

Confidently, Eddie and I stepped onto the Bowlers Bar balcony. Grinning at each other, we grabbed the rope and shook it, hearing the bell ring out to signal the start of the day's play.

Printed in Great Britain
by Amazon

40899971R00101